# Global Crossfire

## *Books by Stephen L. Thompson*

### The Crossfire Series

Colorado Crossfire
International Crossfire
Israeli Crossfire
Believer's Crossfire
Spirit Crossfire
Faith Crossfire
Chinese Crossfire
Texas Crossfire
Dark Crossfire
Island Crossfire
Jagged Crossfire
Violent Crossfire
Russian Crossfire
Nuclear Crossfire
End Times Crossfire
Revelation Crossfire
Gates of Hell Crossfire
Assassin's Crossfire
Global Crossfire
Far East Crossfire

### The SFO Series

Station Force One – Onset

# Global Crossfire

## *"So do not fear, for I am with you"*

**Stephen L. Thompson**

# Global Crossfire

The Crossfire Team has repelled the first two attacks from the Albatross organization with a vengeance. Now they await the next effort from the Anti-Christ's military arm.

After Russia attacks the Sword God sends the team against the Albatross Empire. A surprising result to this conflict is the emergence of a new ally in the battle of the Saints of Christ against Satan and the Demonic.

-       Stephen L. Thompson

# Global Crossfire

**Published by**
Stephen L. Thompson
Facebook.com/CrossfireNovelSeries

ISBN- 978-1-943879-27-4

Published in the United States of America

# Foreword

### *To my Christian readers –*

The Crossfire continuing series of action-adventure novels include depictions of violence which are unusual in Christian literature. It would be nice if there were no conflict or violence in our world. But we live in a time when evil is increasing instead of diminishing, when some men seem to be controlled by selfishness, madness, or evil forces. When the enemies of decent mankind are bent on subjugation of other men and women, righteous men and women must stand against evil. The yoke of oppression is not lifted by prayer alone. God is our shepherd and we are his sheep. As long as there are wolves about, God will use some of us as sheep dogs to defend the rest of us. These stories are about people like that and the forces they fight against. The stories describe violence because it occurs in the real world and it is active in the lives of all people whether they recognize it or not.

### *To my non-Christian readers –*

The Crossfire series include depictions of spiritual warfare and spiritual activity with which the non-Christian reader may not be familiar. These stories describe the realms and activities of both God and Satan because they're real and active in the lives of all people whether they recognize it or not.

*Steve Thompson*

# CHAPTER ONE

It was a beautiful day in the south of France until death came suddenly in the form of concentrated rifle fire that knocked men off their feet before they could make a move. Others died from heavy machine gun fire and several more were killed by RPG grenades.

Good men died without knowing why they had been killed. Mark Connelly knew why and hadn't been able to stop it. The battle had started without any warning. The incoming firepower had been pre-sighted and delivered with military precision, well-coordinated for maximum damage and overall psychological effect.

Sarah had dropped to the ground behind a battered trash dumpster before bullets reached her location. Her experience and training warned her as the first enemy round was fired. Her life as a Mossad field agent and assassin still ruled her reactions in combat situations and that was also why she had been standing close to the dumpster before the firing started. But, regardless of her abilities, the volume of fire from several different vantage points kept her on the ground. She couldn't attempt to fire back without attracting the shooters and probably getting killed herself.

Three members of the Police SWAT unit did fire back at the aggressors with submachine guns without visible success. Their actions did draw the attention of an angry 50-caliber heavy machine gun which ate up the cinder blocks in the wall they were behind and shredded all three men.

Keeping her face on the dirty concrete, she sensed more than felt some of the heavy 50-cal rounds pass just above her back. She really wished God had let them use the force generators, but that wasn't to be this time. Not raising her head, she let her eyes search for her husband, Mark Connelly. She saw the former U.S. Navy SEAL off to her left, crouching behind a mound of broken concrete slabs and firing rifle grenades at the enemy. The effect was to draw heavy return fire which was hellish in volume and accuracy, but it drew it away from the Frenchmen. Mark ducked behind more debris to shield himself from the incoming fire.

The frustration and anger building in Sarah's gut needed to be let out. She keyed her CommNet and got hold of Jack Malone. "Jack! They've got us pinned down and they have heavy weapons, 50-cal machine guns and RPGs! Can we please get some air support?"

Jack's voice was clear and obviously mad about the ambush. "The Formidable is on its way, ETA is ten seconds. Stay down!"

Sarah felt, more than heard, the deep power emanations from the huge war bird. The Albatross warriors were firing from an area two square city blocks in size. A dozen rifles and a ground-to-air missile were fired up at the huge aircraft. Suddenly, the team members were slammed around and partially deafened by the simultaneous subterranean explosion of four 2,000-pound JDAM bombs delivered by the Formidable. Suddenly that entire two block area literally exploded into the air while hundreds of aimed and accurate 20 mm rounds decimated anything still living on the ground around the area which was now exploding with fire as it rose above them.

Sarah was again bounced off the ground as the huge mass of burning land fell back to earth. She saw two fighter jets as they attacked the Formidable only to explode right after their missiles blew up short of their target. Three other fighters turned tail and ran. None of them escaped the missiles fired from the Formidable. The Formidable made three more passes strafing the enemy with six of its ten, 20-millimeter cannons. After that, nothing moved again on that side of the line between the Crossfire Team and the agents of the Albatross.

After the ground quit shaking and jerking as a result of the falling land mass, Mark cautioned everyone to keep cover until they could ensure the threat had been neutralized. No one argued with his advice this time.

Rob, their pilot, called the all clear in from the Formidable and the remaining troops moved out to check their comrades and see if any of them survived. Rob sat the Formidable down near the troops but stayed on board to watch for any new efforts by the Albatross to attack them.

Mark gathered the five members of the Crossfire Team and they prayed their thanks to Father Yahveh and to Yahshua for His protection. The two other groups weren't as fortunate. The French Police had lost eleven out of sixteen members because they hadn't listened to Mark's advice to fall back from what was obviously going to be a military battle.

The twenty-two-man French Home Guard had been completely wiped out. Mark thought back trying to understand why all this death and destruction had happened.

------------------------******------------------------

During the late afternoon hours, the five members of the Crossfire Team had met with the sixteen-man French SWAT team in a remote and seemingly deserted beach in Southern France as requested.

The Angel Rose had delivered a message from the Most High and the team had left their new base on the "Sword" and was dropped off by helicopter. The appearance of any demons might have been bad intelligence, except it was God who had put them there. They looked around the desolated land left by a recent demolishment of a huge old hotel. Three miles away in two directions were beaches or towns teeming with locals and tourists to the south of France.

The one French Officer that spoke English was less than grateful for the presence the three females as part of the American team. Sarah was used to that type of male snobbery and ignored the Frenchmen completely even though she could speak French. Alexis and Su Li just shook their head at such rude attitudes. Mark and David were trying to understand what the French Police were here for on this deserted beach and why they had requested their help.

The one English-speaking Frenchman told them that the Crossfire Team had been called (by a governmental official, done against the desires of the Police) simply due to some impossible demonic involvement. Then he then mentioned that they were here to stop and arrest several members of the Albatross on a tip, an anonymous tip at that.

At that point Mark realized it was a trap. He told the sixteen-man SWAT team police force and their twenty-two French "Home Guard" backup (people most of which didn't even have rifles and none had body armor) to drop back because this was bound to be a military action and even their SWAT team wasn't prepared for war. The French officers scoffed at this advice. That's when hell on Earth had broken out.

---------------------------\*\*\*\*\*\*---------------------------

Mark's memory caught up to the present. Standing there in the shattered beach front with the smells of war wafting by, Mark knew that there wasn't much the Team could do to console the French. They were about to walk to the Formidable when one of the distraught French Policemen sought out Mark. Bitterly complaining, in broken English, he implied that the French losses would not have occurred if the Crossfire Team had fought back like the French had.

Mark felt sorry for the confused Frenchman. The man was grieving and striking out to share his pain. Trying to explain the reality of a military combat ambush would be a waste of words right then. The other French police supported their friend and began to call Mark and the other team members' cowards.

Mark shrugged and turned to walk away when the man grabbed Mark's arm to turn him around, presumably to fight.

Mark began to pray that Almighty God would show him how to peacefully resolve the situation as he turned back. Mark wasn't worried about fighting, he simply didn't want to hurt or embarrass the smaller man.

The Frenchman held his right fist cocked back ready to strike but his face was a frozen sight. His jaw had dropped and his eyes were large with confusion.

Mark realized his silver armor and sword had appeared when he had prayed. Ignoring the Frenchman, he used his CommNet, "All sword bearers, armor up now!"

As David, Alexis, Sarah, and Su Li's armor and swords appeared, Mark called Rob and told him to button up his plane and lift off. As the Formidable rose into the air, Mark got hold of the comm center on the "Sword", their ship off the coast of southern France. Ethan Reaper took Mark's call on the first ring. "Mark, I've got a portal opening up two hundred yards east of your position. Roughly twenty demons headed your way. I'll let you know if more exit the portal, Reaper out."

Mark liked the young man's "to the point" briefness. "Okay team, twenty bad spirits headed our way from the East. Protect the French survivors, Connelly out."

Turning to the stunned Frenchmen he said commandingly, "Stay together, we will try to protect you but you must do as I say. What is coming is worse than what happened before!"

As if emphasizing Mark's comment, the first demon came pounding around a pile of debris. It was a horrible, terrorizingly large one, probably seven-foot-tall with blood red eyes and a snout full of fangs and razor-sharp black teeth. It had four arms, each hand holding a large black sword. Everything about the creature was repulsive, even its smell which wafted off of its ugly, blotchy skin. The demon was obviously very strong and powerful and it was shouting curses in French which didn't affect Mark at all since he didn't understand French and the words had no power over him.

The Frenchmen were either frozen in fear or crouching and screaming as the demon approached with death in its eyes.

Mark stepped between the demon and the Frenchmen and blocked or dodged the four swords. Timing out the motions of the four arms Mark stepped toward the demon as he swung his glowing sword in a quick overhand. This cleanly lopped off two of the creature's arms. Knowing many more demons were coming, he simply spun to his right and back handed his blade beheading the demon, ending the battle in two strokes.

A second, slightly smaller demon skittered on six legs toward the Frenchmen with death on its mind. Su Li ran up behind the demon and kicked it in its rear side to distract it from attacking the Frenchmen. She dodged two sword attacks from the infuriated creature and then stepped inside its defense. This confused the demon since no one but another demon ever tried to get closer to it.

Su Li simply ran her sword through the demon as she stood eye-to-eye with it. The demon wailed a mournful sound as it evaporated. Su Li walked over to Mark with demon stain running off of her golden armor. "We took care of the others." Suddenly both of their armor and swords faded from view and Ethan called to announce that the portal had closed.

Mark walked over to the Frenchmen and told them that the demons were no longer a problem and that it was safe to leave now. The English speaking man was still shaking, but he held out his hand and shook Mark's hand. "I don't know how to thank you for saving us from those hideous things. You and your whole team are not cowards but brave warriors, we were wrong and we are humbled. I am very sorry we offended you." Then he turned and walked away.

Mark called Jack as the Formidable settled back to Earth to pick them up. "What was this all about? We need to talk."

# CHAPTER TWO

The opulent room displayed the absolute best choices in expensive furniture and appointments available. Real crystal, silver and gold highlights adorned polished oak, rosewood, and teak.

The room shouted quietly of wealth and power and prestige. It shouted very discretely of course, showcasing the owner's elitism by their casual dismissal of their worldly trappings. This is a tricky bit of elitism which can only be accomplished by having the most expensive and therefore most exclusive things which one could act completely uncaring about.

The man seated at the ornate desk radiated subdued evil power under tight control. His physique was muscular and his face was a chiseled work of surgical perfection.

His black eyes dominated his face; the set of his jaw dared anyone to question his orders.

The work done on his face had removed his Arabic features, but apparently had done nothing to hide the burning anger in his soul caused by the slave-dominated history of his race.

The name he used was Hiram Windsor but everyone called him "Lord". His word was absolute law and no one defied him on pain of a quick and, usually, cruel death.

Hiram Windsor was the supreme leader of the Albatross Complex. Normally he would be deeply involved in the many worldwide efforts by the Albatross Empire.

All of the Albatross' operations were scorched earth missions. Their targets died horribly cruel deaths. The eviler their dispatching was, the more public they made them. Everyone died, men, women, children, babies. The Albatross was feared world-wide, yet remained a secret. Hiram Walker conceived of ever more vicious ways to destroy a whole town or city and leave it as a warning of their wrath. Their virtual unknown and unfindable factor made the tales and rumors about them grow with every action.

At the present moment he was livid with anger and was intently focusing his interest. He was concerned with not only what happened but he wanted to understand the underlying reasons why his efforts in destroying the people of the Crossfire Team had failed so far. He listened to the group leader assigned to the latest naval efforts. This man had been very accomplished up until this disastrous event, which was his last assignment forever.

Hiram had seen what little satellite coverage was available on the destruction of his naval vessels. Even at the high angle view his keen mind recoiled as the Crossfire ship obliterated his destroyer by ramming into it at high speed with no apparent damage to itself. He was not a blind guide and knew that there was either a new technology that his organization wasn't aware of yet or a supernatural power at work.

Hiram knew he was the most highly trained man in the Albatross Empire and therefore the most qualified agent. So, frustrated by his men's lack of progress against this team he decided that he would investigate them himself.

He organized the many groups and on-going efforts so that the Albatross would be properly managed in their death-dealing missions during his preoccupation with the Crossfire Team.

He started with every scrap of Elint or electronic intelligence he could get on the team's history. He was surprised by the wealth of information and the complete lack of "how" they did whatever they were involved in.

Hiram changed tactics and listened to the two team leaders of the Crossfire Team as they explained the events to various officials and committees. It quickly became clear that these two men were highly talented but not exceptionally so. It was the power of their Hebrew-Christian God that was fighting through them to achieve their miraculous victories. That changed everything!

Hiram Windsor knew about Yahveh. He had contended with the followers and the messengers of the God of the Jews and the Christians before. He also sourly remembered that he had not always come away a winner in those battles. If he believed his own press, which he did not, the Albatross had won most of those conflicts. In reality they had never won a single battle against Yahveh.

This greatly complicated his challenge and he needed to pray to his god as to how to defeat this spiritually protected team of enemies. Satan was fickle and not to be trusted, but if you achieved his goals, life could be victorious in many ways. Hiram was confident he would come out on top in his conflict with the Crossfire Team.

# CHAPTER THREE

During a break, Jack felt led to pray to Yahveh and Yahshua, giving thanks for the "Sword", the magnificent ship that God had given the team. Of course, calling something that is seven hundred and seventy-seven feet long weighing over 45,000 tons, merely a ship was like calling an army just a bunch of people.

Its sheer size was daunting. It was closer along the lines of a heavy cruiser. As he prayed and praised Yahshua, and the Father, Jack had a visitation. He looked up and saw Raquel the Archangel sitting on nothing, simply grinning at him.

This was the first time that Jack had seen Raquel grinning. The angel looked humorously at him, "Jack, the Father knows how much you love him for giving you this ship thus protecting your team as well as the land of His chosen people, Israel. There are so many people on this ship that are following His Son and profess their love for Him that the Father's love is here all the time. Also, with so many of your naval crew being not only Jewish but Jewish sailors, men and women who have a solid belief and daily need for their God. These people love him because He is their ever faithful Jehovah Jireh."

This whole time Raquel continued to smile at Jack. Jack finally said, "What are you grinning about?"

Raquel said, "The fact that I know something in your Earthly realm that you do not. It is something so powerful that is necessary for your survival. This ship offers an additional dimension of combat of which you need to be aware. Jack raised his eyebrows and looked hard at Raquel, "What do you mean?"

Raquel posed a question, "You have this huge ship with all openings sealed against the sea. There are no portholes or external antennas on this ship. Do you know why that is?"

Jack responded by saying, "I assume it is to keep our radar signature at a minimum".

"Much more than that", said Raquel, "Actually, this ship is also the largest submarine the world has never seen." At that, Jack shook his head as he stood up. "No one ever said anything about this ship being capable of submerging!"

The angel said, "That is because this ship was built in such compartmentalized secrecy, that most of the people involved in it did not know about all of it. Consider this, it is powered by 3 nuclear reactors and has no weak spots in the hull, such as portholes."

Jack sat there for a minute trying to process what he just heard. "Where are the controls to operate it as a submarine?" Raquel smiled as he replied, "Get Su Li, she will know where the controls are located."

Jack said, "She is a pilot, not a naval officer."

Raquel chuckled and said, "Ask her if she remembers why the Shrew can be either a commercial aircraft or a fighter aircraft. If need be, remind her about the Canard wings." Then the Archangel grinned again and faded out of sight.

Jack could tell Raquel was enjoying his angelic insight too much. He decided to explore this new possibility immediately and went in search of Commander Hugh Kelly, who was second in command of the ship. His rating was Executive Officer or, in Navy shorthand, the XO. As Jack walked toward the portal, he used the CommNet to call Mark, Su Li, and Laura and asked them to accompany him.

After they gathered together and headed for the bridge, Mark asked, "What's going on?"

Jack looked at him and grinned. He said, "You don't suffer from claustrophobia, do you?" Mark looked at him and said, "What? Jack you know me better than that. As a Navy SEAL, you know I don't have a problem with enclosed spaces."

Jack looked forward and replied, "That's good, as I just found out, that the "Sword" can also operate as a submarine."

To say the others were shocked was an understatement. Arriving at the bridge, Jack requested permission for them to enter and were so granted.

As they moved forward, Su Li asked Jack, "Why am I here? "

Jack said, "Because you apparently know the secrets to what we are seeking."

Hugh Kelly showed up at that moment and Jack asked, "Did you have any clue that this ship can also be used as a submarine?"

Commander Kelly, looked at Jack and said, "Hmm.... I wondered about that. But, since there was no Conning tower control room or torpedo bays, I dismissed the idea."

Jack turned to Su Li. "The Archangel Raquel said that since you know how the "Shrew" could be a Bizjet and a fighter jet as needed, you would know why the "Sword" could be a surface ship and also operate as a submarine as needed."

Su Li nodded. "I'll bet he mentioned the Canard wings too."

Jack smiled, "He did."

She turned to the XO. "Commander Kelly, where is the primary instrument control point which controls the movement of the "Sword" over the sea?"

As he thought about that, Su Li added, "In other words, where is the driver's seat?"

Nodding his head, he led them across the bridge to a single seaman who sat in front of a dozen screens with a combination wheel which was attached to a post rising up from the deck that altered direction and velocity of the huge ship. The XO introduced Yeoman Peters to Su Li who asked if she could sit in his position. At a nod from the XO, the yeoman set the ship on autopilot and gave his seat to the young woman. He took a position just to her right and slightly behind her. Su Li tested the controls and then asked the Yeoman where the one control he never used was. With no hesitation he pointed to a large orange lever on the far right of the console. "Where is the other unused control?"

Yeoman Peters shook his head. "The orange control is the only unused one. I believe it is a test control."

She then asked if there were any other test controls at his station.

He shook his head. "The Master test control is at the XO's position. I was told these controls are only used during dry dock configuration tests."

Su Li stood up and gave the yeoman his seat back. She turned to the XO. "Commander Kelly, would it be possible to bring the ship to a full stop?" The XO looked perplexed but said, "Helm, give me a solution for an immediate full stop."

Yeoman Peters checked his screens and talked to Radar/Sonar. "We are cleared for an immediate full stop, XO."

The XO nodded, "Make it happen."

Su Li smiled, "I believe we could do this at speed, but since we've never tried it before, I thought it would be prudent to tread lightly." She looked at Hugh and told him to move the orange handled control at his position first, as it was probably a master control that would allow the other lever to work.

Hugh went to his position and moved the orange lever to the lower position. The net observable result was an orange indicator light started to blink at both positions.

The XO spoke to Yeoman Peters, "Move your orange lever."

When that lever was lowered to the operating position many things changed. The Yeoman's station changed many of its screens and the control wheel moved outward from its position in the console so that it now also controlled several massive diving surfaces to regulate the vertical position of the ship in the water. Both indicator lights quit blinking and glowed solidly.

Yeoman Peters grimaced and looked at Commander Kelly. "Sir, I am neither trained nor rated to operate the ship in this configuration."

Kelly looked at Jack. "This was your surprise; how can we use it?"

Mark grinned, "I think we have a solution. One of the Sensitive Operations Group that joined the Crossfire Team was a nuclear sub driver in the U.S. Navy before he was called by God to join us. His service record was exemplary. His name is Ian Mitchell. Also, he is a sword bearer."

The Commander looked speculative and nodded his head and ordered the ship to return to normal surface configuration and previous course and speed for the present.

# CHAPTER FOUR

Ian Mitchell rushed into the gym and spotted Jack working on a technique with Su Li. He ran up to them and loudly exclaimed "This is FANTASTIC!"

As a long time teacher of Martial Arts, Jack was able to break his focus without letting his foot strike Su Li's head where it had been about to do just that. Even though she had a protective headgear, this probably saved Ian from a bad beating at her hands later. Jack straightened up and looked at the man calmly, "What is so fantastic Mr. Mitchell?"

It suddenly entered the young man's over stimulated mind what he had done and he snapped to attention and saluted Jack as he apologized to his commanding General for interrupting them. He also included Su Li in his apology. He knew she was one of the most dangerous women in the world. His face was already flushed so it didn't give away his embarrassment.

Su Li stepped over to the man and said, "This had bettered be worth it." It was obvious that she meant it.

Ian stayed at attention. "Yes Ma'am it is." He looked at Jack. General Sir, studying the documents on operating the "Sword" as a submarine I discovered an operational parameter that is really fantastic. In the submerged role this ship can travel underwater at a speed of over 250 knots per hour. That's roughly 300 miles per hour! Submerged!"

Su Li was surprised, "Considering the friction of the boat's hull through the water how can that be real?"

Ian smiled, "Because there is no friction. This ship is equipped with super-cavitation using a preceding air bubble."

Jack had reread Ian's records and knew he was well qualified in this area of science. He held a PhD in Nautical Engineering in fact. "Say that's true, we still need full speed tests before we could use it safely."

Ian shook his head. "The U.S. Navy already ran them six months ago. I've got the records. It worked perfectly for over two hundred miles in the Pacific Ocean last year. The entire run only took one hour"

Jack smiled at Su Li. "I guess this fact was worth the interruption."

Su Li slowly nodded her head and smiled at Ian. This removed a semi-serious concern he had about staying healthy long enough to actually get to drive the boat

Jack called a Core Team meeting and finished up with Su Li's training.

Forty minutes later he met with the Core Team in the new War Room on the Sword.

Jack stood six feet, four inches tall and had developed a solid, muscular two-hundred-pound body due to the constant training and combat the team had been waging over the last five years. He had short cut blonde hair and intense blue-green eyes. As the anointed Priest and leader of the team he carried himself as the authority figure of the team.

Jack explained Ian Mitchell's discovery and the unexpected benefits it offered. He then asked one question of the assembled cast. How will these advantages help them since the Force Generator protected them from anything and essentially made them invisible on the surface anyway?

Mark Connelly looked the part of the military leader of the Crossfire Team. His two hundred and twenty-pound weight was balanced over his six-foot, two-inch frame. He looked like an ideal Marine on a recruiting poster and fulfilled his role with solid grit and determination which complimented Jack's more fluid strength with the active rock-hard body that allowed him to muscle through most confrontations with maximum effort. He had a good-looking face with brown eyes and a mass of black hair that spoke of honor.

Mark felt that his hardheaded dependency on his own mental and physical capabilities had finally learned to bow to the superiority of the Father and Son. As he cleared his mind in preparation to ask God about this question, he received a Word. He immediately remembered that God already knew the situation and the outcome and He had simply been waiting for Mark to humble himself and ask.

In the Core Team meeting he spoke up, "This submarine capability is important because, first, if there are no coincidences and an Angel told you about it which is the same thing as God telling you Himself, this alone makes it important now. Second, there could be a future time when we can't rely on the Force Generator. I don't know why or when but I was made aware of that possibility. And thirdly, it provides us with an advantage in close-in personnel operations that the Generator can't fulfill such as uncloaked covert exits and recoveries."

Jack agreed with Mark's reasoning and sought any other inputs. He didn't get any more input, just a lot of questions about the new capabilities the submarine mode gave them.

David Zahavy was eight years older than Jack and Mark. He was a well-dressed man and after fourteen years as a field agent and training manager with the Israeli Mossad was very competent in all forms of spy work and combat. His light brown hair framed a classical Jewish face and his brown eyes never missed a detail.

David suggested, "Since we're in the mid-Atlantic why don't we try it at speed?"

Jack looked at Ian sitting behind him. "Are you ready to ride the bull, Ian?"

Ian nodded enthusiastically, "Yes Sir!"

Jack made a call to the Captain and secured his agreement to the trial. Jack and Ian went to the bridge while the rest of the core team watched via monitor.

On the bridge as they waited until the "Sword" was brought to a halt, Jack spoke to David out loud, "David, right now I would dearly love to have the software the Mossad's "Sand Snakes" use for course availability and control."

David came back with, "I'll see what I can do in cooperation with Ethan."

Yeoman Peters stepped away from the pilot's seat and motioned to Commander Mitchell to take control. Once Ian reverted to a naval posting his rank as Commander was reinstated. As they passed, the yeomen whispered, "Please, don't break her."

Completely understanding the passion and sincerity in the plea, Ian smiled and whispered back, "Don't worry, I will treat her with the greatest respect."

Both Captain Conners and XO Hugh Kelly stood to the rear of Ian as the "ship" became a submarine when Ian lowered the large Orange lever on the side of his control console. All the screens changed and the main screen showed the surface of the ocean in front of the "boat".

Ian called out, "XO, the board is green, and the boat is secure, ready for diving orders."

The XO responded, "Dive the boat Commander, make your depth eighty feet and level."

Ian came back with, "Aye, aye XO, level at eighty feet." He moved the control yoke downward slightly and the main screen showed the water rising over the deck and then over the camera. An outlined box indicated the depth in feet. It rose to the number 80 and stopped. The hull position indicator showed a small image of the "Sword" in a fore-aft level position.

The XO spoke, "Make your forward speed twenty knots, Commander."

"Aye-aye XO, twenty knots."

Ian moved the control yoke forward until the speed indicator read "20". The front view main screen showed movement of the boat through the sea water. Another screen showed a satellite view and a green line indicating the movement of the submerged "Sword" as well as any obstacles or other surface ships or aircraft.

Ian spoke up, "Permission to test forward speed capability XO."

The XO replied, "Permission granted Commander."

Jack suddenly said, "Belay that order, Commander Mitchell!"

Ian responded, "Yes sir, General Malone! Belaying the speed test."

Both the Captain and the XO stared at Jack. This was a major breech in command structure. Jack turned to the two men, "Captain Conners, Commander Kelly, please forgive me for that slip in protocol. I did not intend to usurp your authority on your ship. But, to prevent any embarrassment or confusion on either of your parts I felt it was critical to bring some information to your attention that I neglected to tell you in the rush of events this afternoon."

The captain, as the senior officer nodded and his visage softened. "Please present that information General."

Jack smiled tightly. "We discovered earlier today that the "Sword" has been equipped with the ability to generate ship-size super-cavitation and reach, fully tested speeds under water of approximately two-hundred and fifty knots while submerged. I believe that is the speed Commander Mitchell was about to attempt to achieve."

Commander Kelly looked shocked, "Good God, man! At those speeds we would be two miles past anything we destroyed before we knew it was there!"

Ian spoke up, "XO can I speak to that concern, please?" The Captain overrode the XO, "Go ahead, Commander Mitchell."

Ian spoke carefully, "Sirs, that concern was taken into consideration in the original design and development plans. During high-speed maneuvers the new laser sonar will locate any obstruction to the ship's travel and would automatically reduce the speed if needed. The enhanced sonar can detect an object the size of a dingy in excess of five miles. This is also backed up by a combination Satellite radar/deep probe capability that can "see" three miles straight down from the surface of the sea when overhead. This is from a low satellite orbit. We won't hit anything Sirs, unless you want to and then we can be very precise in doing so."

The XO had calmed down during Ian's explanation. "How long do we have to wait to acquire this satellite and its deep probe capabilities, Commander?"

Ian replied, "No time at all XO. This is a dedicated satellite system that is always available to this ship. It's actually one of sixteen satellites lofted into low orbit when this ship made its sea trials. The whole system of satellites is repositioned as this ship moves. So we can go anywhere the ship can submerge on Earth and a satellite is always standing by. See the satellite symbol on the screen here?" Ian indicated a solidly lit symbol of a satellite with a lightning bolt descending from it.

Hugh Kelly smiled and shook his head, "Another bloody impossibility which seem to follow you and your team,

General. Tell me Commander, how can the satellites reposition themselves? That would take huge amounts of rocket propellant that a low orbit satellite could not carry."

Ian nodded his head, "That would be true XO if they used rockets to move them. These satellites use solar power and a new ion drive to do the job. A fact proven by the fact the satellites were over the Atlantic for the sea trials and they are now over the Pacific Ocean."

Jack smiled back. "XO, these things aren't impossible, we're just blessed by God. He is the one that sent an Archangel to tell me about the "Sword's" submarine capability. You should get to know Him better, I know He loves you and I'd bet He even likes you."

The XO nodded "An "Arch" Angel no less." he turned to Ian. "Commander, resume your speed test. Make your speed two hundred and fifty knots at two hundred feet."

Ian responded, "Aye-aye XO, two hundred and fifty knots at two hundred feet."

# CHAPTER FIVE

The "Sword" more than lived up to its test documentation and maintained its speed for ninety-plus minutes. The video screens showed the immense speed of the ship as it sped through the sea like a bullet fired in anger.

But there was nothing to see for most of the people on the ship and, thanks to the Force Generator field, there was nothing to feel. So the majority of the crew had no sensation of the watery world flashing by only a few feet away at three hundred miles per hour.

Jack talked to the Captain for a while and then excused himself and went back to the Crossfire team's quarters. He never realized when Ian had returned the boat to a normal cruising speed due to a Russian Trawler, or better known as a "spy boat" ahead near their path. Jack wondered what the Russian spy boat thought of the "Sword" as it passed their position. A submarine is one thing, but a submarine the size of a battleship?

On the bridge several alarms sounded and the XO called out to Commander Mitchell, "That's an attack alarm! What's the source?"

Ian was doing four things at once and still was able to respond, "Underwater missile attack! I am tracking four missiles from the Russian Trawler, XO. Turning into the missile track to give a minimum profile and deploying counter measures. Since the Force Generator is active the missiles cannot harm the ship but you can bet that Trawler is recording everything we're doing. They have also now fired four ASROC air-to-sea missiles. Orders XO?"

Commander Kelly nodded his head. "Weapons, use the deck laser to cut off all antennas and the prop shafts on that ship, now destroy any additional attack missiles. I am shutting down the force generator field now. Comm! Blanket the area for all forms of electronic signals communications."

"Commander Mitchell, as quickly as possible, I want to be twenty feet away from that ship on the surface.

Boarding troops, I want twenty sailors on deck as soon as possible after the ship broaches the surface. Be prepared to board a hostile crewed ship. Defend yourselves against attack, kill enemy combatants, and capture officers. Do these things quickly because these buggers have a penchant for blowing themselves up rather than surrendering, Chop, chop ladies and gentlemen, the clock is running!"

Ian cranked up the speed and surfaced at a speed of sixty knots and brought the "Sword" to a sudden halt using the MHD drive systems placing the "Sword" twenty feet from the leeward side of the trawler. To the crew of the trawler the huge ship suddenly appeared next to their ship which was rocking about due the water displacement by the larger ship. Ian reached over and lifted the orange lever and reported, "the ship is in surface mode, Yeoman Peters you have the conn. XO, permission to join the boarding party."

As the XO headed out to the deck he responded, "Permission denied Commander, you're too bloody valuable in here!"

The battle for the Trawler was essentially over by the time Hugh got to the deck. A dozen of the Trawler's crew was sprawled in their own blood on the Trawler's deck and four Russian Officers were on their knees with their hands bound behind them. Mark Connelly stepped over to the deck of the smaller ship and looked at the mess. He was talking to Ethan Reaper in the computer center on the "Sword", "Were you able to get everything from the Russian computers?"

Ethan Reaper was a brown haired Caucasian with tattoos up and down both arms. At six feet of height he had transitioned from an expert hacker to working for Charlie Wu in the ComSec Department. His innate talents in sleuthing and computers earned him the head position in ComSec when Charlie and his wife Linda left to be more involved in combat.

Ethan came back, "Yes Sir, I was in time to save their communications logs as well, before their wipe program deleted them."

Very good Major, print the last hours' worth of Russian chit-chat in English for our interrogations of these officers. Is there any reason not to sink this ship as we leave?"

"No need Sir; their own self-destruct charges should do the job for us. You might hustle things a bit as they set it to blow in ten minutes"

Mark got everyone onto the deck of their ship and had it moved a half mile away before the Russian ship blew itself to pieces and sank quickly beneath the sea.

Mark had the Russian officers blindfolded and taken to the brig in sector C. They picked the Captain for the first interrogation. They took off his blindfold and locked his hands to the chair which was bolted to the floor. Mark and Hugh Kelly sat across from him. Mark asked the sailor why his ship fired on their ship. The Captain smirked; in good English he asked a question of his own. "How are you going to explain your attack on a Russian ship, killing its crew and kidnapping its officers before sinking it?"

Commander Kelly answered that one. "First, since no state of war exists between Russia and Israel your firing on us without provocation means either you were told to do this heinous thing by a higher Russian Officer or you did this on your own which makes you a terrorist. Your second attack of four ASROC missiles shows that the first attack was not a mistake.

Mark slowly flipped through his files on the table before him as he studied the Russian Captain across the table. The man's bravado was part ego, part training and part fear.

The Captain smirked again. His ship had been destroyed, but, at least he had destroyed all the records before this infernally fast giant ship had appeared next to them. They let the Trawler explode and sink in unfathomable depth. They had no evidence to convict him, foolish Israelis! He'd be on a plane home by tomorrow with the Israeli President's apologies.

Mark decided to let the air out of the arrogant man. "Captain, I see from your records that you were ordered to attack us by retired Fleet Admiral Nikolayevich, now he is FSB of course and will deny any involvement. This means he will put all blame for firing on us at your doorstep. This means you will be labeled as a terrorist. So you will get to visit Gitmo and be condemned for the rest of your life and back home in Mother Russia your wife Elaina will bear the scorn and derision of being the wife of a traitor. Your little girl will share the guilt for the rest of her life."

Mark looked at a man whose whole future was collapsing before his eyes. "This is your one and only chance to walk out of this a free man with a future for your family and your name. Explain in detail the Russian thinking and planning that allows your actions without concern about reactions from other countries such as all-out war with Israel."

The captain slowly nodded his head. "If you will guarantee asylum for me and my family in Israel I will tell you what you want to know."

Two hours later The Captain was transferred to an aircraft and the custody of Israeli under a code name to prevent retaliation by the Russians or the Anti-Christ-controlled government.

The other three officers were given to the Israeli Government for interrogation with a cover story that there had been an unexplained death of their Captain under interrogation. The lesser officers wouldn't talk because they didn't know anything. Eventually, they would be sent back to Russia as heroes along with the knowledge of their heroic Captain who died rather than give any information to the enemy. An unnoticed side note was the disappearance of the Captain's wife and daughter. These things happened frequently in their country and it was best if one did not pry into things that didn't involve them.

# CHAPTER SIX

Mark sat at his position in the Sword's War Room. He addressed the Core Team and Commander Kelly about the Russian Trawler incident. He looked at the assembled cast of Jack and Laura, Sarah, David and Alexis, Charlie and Linda Wu, Christi Steele, Ethan Reaper, Megan Cole, Carol Moffet, and Elon. Christi's friend, Rachel, was training in Israel to be a spy. Mark was proud of each and every one of the fourteen warriors. He smiled, "You all are aware of the attack by the Russian spy trawler on the Sword. Now you will learn the rest of the story as Paul Harvey used to say. It seems that the Russians are being either controlled or in collaboration with the Albatross Empire which we know now is the military arm for the Anti-Christ, Marco Marino."

"Subtlety, is not a Russian strong point, and is not involved in this case. If the attack on us caused any concerns to anybody other than Israel or the U.S. it would be dismissed by one of those two powers and the whole thing forgotten. We can now declare war between the Crossfire Team and the part of the world ruled by Marino which now includes America and Europe. We made a bold statement to the Albatross that we would do greater damage to the attackers than was done to us. How we do that, and to who? The attack was done by Russia. I would like a consensus on the type and method of our "meaningful" response."

David spoke up, "I understand the situation and recommend we pray and ask God before we rush out and take on the anti-Christ's world. If God agrees then I suggest we make a world class response and we take out the entire Russian spy trawler fleet by ourselves regardless who they are pestering right now."

Commander Kelly laughed, "That could be over two thousand ships and would bring the Russian Bear down on us in spades. I doubt that God wants that."

Laura Malone was a beautiful woman with short cut blonde hair and green eyes. At six-foot-tall she was a good compliment to her husband Jack. She was also a compliment to him in her prayer life and partner in his job as Priest to the team.

Laura spoke up, "Let's pray."

Jack led the prayers for God's guidance and leading.

The response was instant and selective. Out of the entire Crossfire Team, Jack saw that there was a puzzling group made up out of him, Laura, Mark, Sarah, David, Alexis, Rabbi Epstein, Rabbi Ben Chanan, and Carol Moffet. The two Rabbis weren't even a part of the team. Knowing innately that God doesn't make mistakes Jack settled back to see what revelation was forthcoming.

They all found themselves in a large room with heavenly views outside the large windows. Everyone was looking around at each other when Yahshua appeared before them. He held out his nail-scarred hands and spoke. *"My peace I give you. I wanted each of you here at this time so I can make everyone more heavenly minded. Up until now you have operated out of the mindset and knowledge you were given during your previous life and during your time since you became a team for the Father. Still, much of your present mindset is Earthly and flesh-based because that is all that you have had to work with until now."*

*"My guidance for your latest contemplated return strike is, no, don't do what you are thinking of doing. If you could accomplish only a part of what you are considering, it will thrust your group into a direct confrontation with national powers on a level I have not anointed for you. Your spiritual roles, individually or corporately do not lend themselves to being or acting as a world power. The Crossfire Team is not mentioned in the scriptures because that is beyond anything you have been anointed to do."*

*"As you enter this latest accountability of war with the Father's enemies you will need to not only act with more wisdom but you need to understand wisdom differently to act as God's Hands here on Earth. With several special exceptions, I will not allow you to act on the national level, But, because of certain events, I need you to understand on a level above that."*

*"To begin with, each of you needs to understand that life on Earth is truly only a small segment of your life with*

*the Father. It was a time of trials and testing which all of you are now done with. Your roles from now on will allow you to see a clearer picture of the Father's universe and all life within it. Your involvement with Satan and the Demonic Realm and now, entire Earthly powers such as Russia, demands that you start moving into and understanding your roles on a larger stage."*

*"In your first view, I am going to alter your mind's view of life to how you view existence. No longer will the death of the body be seen as very important or as a dividing time in your life, it is only a step to a new reality where time and distance are not limits, only relevant data."*

Jack took a deep breath as he realized that his ages old concerns about the end of his fleshly body or his time on Earth had evaporated and didn't exist in his mind any more. His heart jumped as he thought about his relationship with Laura and realized his love and concern for her were still as strong as before. The Lord's voice in his mind reminded him that the Father is love and those concepts are eternal. Jack's eyes turned to the love of his life on Earth and seeing her smiling at him he smiled back at her. It was obvious that her first thought had been of him and their love.

*"Now I will increase your concepts of faith, wisdom, and My Kingdom. You will understand things you have not known before about all the relationships each of you have had with people, angels, the demonic; and will continue to have on the Earth. Your commitment to God our Father and my role as your Savior will assume the correct balance in your existence and how that relates to others. This will balance you as you move forward in your understanding of things. As is written in My Word in Proverbs 8, Wisdom is the key to life. Go in my peace and begin to see everyone in the Father's love, as I would."*

The hall and the Lord faded away and the seven members of the core Team found themselves back in the War Room on the Sword. As they tried out their new understanding they relaxed, feeling a mature wisdom that hadn't been there before.

Jack looked at David and asked, "Would you like to re-think your solution for a response?"

David nodded his head. His new understanding of his place in the Heavenly Father's Kingdom would definitely require a new paradigm. He realized he was now viewing the operation of the Russian country as a whole including their rationale and functioning of the geo-political state and their military. Limited areas of knowledge and comprehension were opened to his mind that he hadn't had before. The new capabilities were truth from God. David now felt compassion for the lives of all the Russian people and even the members of the Albatross Empire. He realized for the first time how his actions truly affected other people. He saw a sample of the operations of demons and angels on and for people and how that affected the course of events in all of the lives that were impacted.

He noticed that he more easily reviewed and manipulated facts and data and was better able to extrapolate the outcomes. He was also acutely aware that all of this input and mind work was because of the Holy Spirit within him and he gave all of the glory for his abilities to Yahveh. David was quite aware that it wasn't him or his abilities that could be praised, but only Yahveh and Yahshua that empowered him. He also realized that while his knowledge was increased and now more positively God-oriented, he knew far less than the lowliest of the angels. He looked up at Jack and asked, "Could I have a short time to rethink my response?" Jack agreed.

Laura was silent as her thoughts encompassed the team's role in God's plan for all mankind. It was a very miniscule part, necessitated by Satan's illegal moving of demons into the human dimension and God's use their team, along with eleven other such teams around the world, to counter those actions. Miniscule it might be, but it was still critical to the Father's plans. She sat in awe and amazement at the immense, yet perfect plan that the Father had created millennia ago for the human race.

With her new view and her new knowledge of the Father's plan, she considered what response the team should give to send a powerful signal to the Albatross Empire and the Russians which would be aligned with God's desire to provide salvation to all people on Earth.

Realizing that the Holy Spirit within her already knew what would be correct, she relaxed and communed with the

Holy Spirit by praying quietly in her prayer language. After discerning the correct answer, she spoke up. "We need to take our response against the top level of the Albatross Empire. For three reasons,

First, they were the ones who ordered the strike against our ship. Second, they aren't worried about any reprisal because they work for Satan and lastly, it is the Albatross that wants us dead. The Russians aren't smart enough to really care about this one ship as yet."

Jack added, "Albatross already knew we would not be damaged. They want us to strike against the Russians to pervert our mission for God. Very good Laura, do you all agree that we should respond against the leaders of the Albatross?"

The assembled members of the Core Team agreed completely.

Alexis added, "Having tried to introduce all-out war between us and the Russians, our response needs to be such that the leaders of the Albatross will understand the severity of such a response. We need to cut the head off of the snake with a measured violence that will make any new leaders avoid conflict with God in the future."

Jack sampled the mood of the group and asked, "Okay what should that response be?"

Mark threw out some concepts out for consideration. "First thing to consider is that after we eliminated the RHONE, the previous military arm of Marco Marino's, he used the world's resources and made an agreement with the Albatross. If we do the same thing to the Albatross, he will probably just hire someone else. Secondly, if we go after the Albatross' hardware they will just replace it. Lastly, Albatross is largely unknown to the people of the world. Whatever we do to them will be covered up by the Anti-Christ controlled press and we will be painted as the bad guys."

Laura laughed, "I realize the results the last time I suggested this, but, why don't we seek God's advice in prayer?"

This time the same team as last time found themselves in a Heavenly classroom facing Hugo, the training angel. A wise face on an ageless body gave Hugo a mentor look. The new wisdom that Yahshua had blessed the team with let them all wait quietly in peace until the angel decided to speak to them.

Hugo nodded his head after receiving instructions that only he could hear. "Greetings Warriors, your confusion is understandable. I am here to help you bridge the gap between having more knowledge and being able to use that knowledge. It is simply a case of learning how to apply it. So, the first thing I am going to do is instill peace in each one of you."

A relaxing feeling settled over the team members and the two Rabbis.

"You now have the option to put your question into God's perspective by yourselves as to what the Father would do. Focus on what God would want you to do, rather than trying to resolve it in your own wisdom."

Jack asked Hugo, "Why this particular group of individuals?"

Hugo smiled, "Because this is primarily a spiritual leadership revelation. The only one I've ever seen by the way. Jack, you and Laura are the anointed spiritual leaders of the Crossfire Team and need this revelation to understand the Most High's plan as you lead the others as priests."

"Mark and Sarah are the military leaders of the team and equally need to understand the bigger picture of the plan to lead correctly."

"David and Alexis are the Social and Political leaders and also need to understand to lead in those sectors."

"Carol's "unique" function for the team needs to understand, as the rest of you now do, to correctly interpret the events and meanings of the Matrix for you."

"Rabbi Ben Chanan and Rabbi Epstein are the spiritual references for the team and as such need to be informed as you are."

The Core team and both of the Rabbis found themselves back in the Sword's War Room.

Jack realized that God wanted some communication between the two men and the team before they were returned to their previous positions. "Rabbi Ben Chanan, it seems your association with us has now impacted your life more than we expected."

The older man smiled, "I now understand much more clearly about everything that was needlessly bothering me. I and my office are at your team's service whenever you need me. I thank you all for the most wonderful revelation in my entire life." With that, both Rabbis disappeared.

After that, Jack used his new heightened ability to discern what God wanted to result from their actions rather than what they wanted. He was startled to realize that he had immediately dropped back into his fleshly thinking.

He thought about what the Father wanted. First, He wanted a result that would convince the leaders of the Albatross to cease trying to attack God's chosen warriors because it was wasted effort and a waste of resources. Secondly, God wanted the Albatross leaders to leave God's Kingdom of believers alone because that would bring them into direct conflict with God's warriors, an effort they should realize they couldn't win. Lastly, by His own word God wanted the Crossfire Team to explain these things to said leaders in such a way that they would never forget the lesson. Now, how could the team accomplish God's desires?

A concept grew in Jack's mind that would do all those things. He quickly prayed and asked if what he was considering was in the will of God. Assured that it was acceptable, he spoke up. "God wants us to invade the top level of the Albatross, make the leaders helpless and impotent, explain the futility of combat against God's chosen, and take away something of critical importance to them as a reminder of their powerlessness against God."

Everyone was digesting Jack's information so Jack summed up what the team's required actions were. "We need to identify the leaders and their location. We also need to identify something of critical importance to them and how we can take it from them, permanently."

# CHAPTER SEVEN

Jack looked at the assembly. "All right people, half of you get with Mark and locate and identify the leaders of the Albatross. The rest of you find out what we need to take away from these leaders and report to me."

The research took less than an hour. The new mindsets and access to some heavenly knowledge streamlined the conception process and eliminated all false trails or bad judgments.

Mark summed up the identity question research. "It seems that there are about one hundred and forty second-level managers that control all of the activities and carry out the demands of Hiram Windsor who is the supreme leader of the Albatross Complex. If we are going against the Albatross we going against Hiram Windsor, whom the Holy Spirit says is directly controlled by Satan. Also, his whereabouts is a hidden base at an unknown location. It might take us some time to locate him.

Ethan Reaper's disembodied voice spoke in the air. "Nope, I just found him."

Charlie and Linda had come into the War room. Charlie spoke up. "No way! Linda and I just combed the world's records with Crayton and didn't find a glimmer of the man or his base."

Ethan laughed "You didn't find him because that is what he is hiding. I didn't look for him, I looked for his stuff. I tasked Crayton to find extremely expensive furniture purchases in the last six months based on my assumption this character would have the best of everything. Very few people buy a two million, fifty-six-thousand-dollar desk with eight hundred thousand dollars' worth of upgrades. Even fewer still, have their own henchmen fly thousands of miles to personally pick their purchase up instead having the manufacturer deliver it. In fact, only one did all this recently. "

"I located one of the only manufacturers of such pricy status symbols which is located in the state of Arizona in the U.S. I hacked their records and found a computer entry for this purchase warning *that Mr. Windsor is extremely picky – no blemishes!* I got the "Ship to:" address and thanks to a Royal Air Force's military satellite I watched it being unloaded at a business off of the M25, the "London Orbital Motorway" northeast of London three weeks ago. The building is near the town of Abridge on the A113 or Onger Road. I think I may have even gotten a picture of the mysterious Hiram Windsor himself. As the huge desk was being carefully off loaded from a lorry this finely dressed man comes out of the loading dock area to personally supervise the unloading. I'm sending you the address file and pictures now."

Jack nodded as the Holy Spirit had also told him these conclusions. "Then we also know what we need to take away from him as an eternal reminder. Hiram Windsor's connection to the demonic."

Mark Connelly stared at him. "How do we do that?"

Jack smiled, "Actually, we can't do it, but God can and that is what He wants. Our job will be to confront Hiram and set before him his choices. Remember, he is associated with the ultimate evil but only believes that evil is his only way of life."

Mark nodded his head, "I like it. We don't remove him; we derail him, and leave him without direction from the demonic, sweet!"

Carol had an intelligence beyond her young years. Selected by God to be a Watchman on the Wall for the team she was anointed to interrogate the "matrix" a ninth dimension agenda list that included all the requests of God. This included requests by the demonic forces that were the main assignment for the team. A pretty woman in her early twenties she had a petite figure and black hair with blue eyes and a button nose.

Carol spoke up, "Where do demons come from and what are they?"

Jack answered. "Where do demons come from? Demons are fallen angels, the one-third of the angels in Heaven who chose to serve Satan. Revelation 12:8-9 NKJV. *"But they did not prevail, nor was a place found for them in heaven any longer. So the great dragon was cast out, that serpent of old, called the Devil and Satan, who deceives the whole world; he was cast to the earth, and his angels were cast out with him*."

"Carol, as you know, we are in a spiritual battle with evil spirits; Satan and his fallen angels. Ephesians 6:11, 12, NKJV. "*Put on the whole armor of God that you may be able to stand against the wiles of the devil. For we do not wrestle against flesh and blood, but against principalities, against powers, against the rulers of the darkness of this age, against spiritual hosts of wickedness in the heavenly places.*" When we fight against people with weapons it is people controlled by Satan or by his demonic empire."

"God warns us through His word against trying to communicate with "familiar spirits," or ghosts. In Isaiah 8:19, NASB. "*When they say to you "Consult the mediums and the spiritists who whisper and mutter," should not a people consult their God? Should they consult the dead on behalf of the living*?"

"Evil spirits can perform miracles and signs to deceive. In Revelation 16:14, NKJV. "*For they are spirits of demons, performing signs, which go out to the kings of the earth and of the whole world, to gather them to the battle of that great day of God Almighty.*"

"We do not have to be afraid of demonic impersonations of the living and the dead, if we give our hearts to Yahshua and stay away from such satanic activities as séances, Ouija boards, etc. In 1 John 4:1, 4, NKJV. "*Beloved, do not believe every spirit, but test the spirits, whether they are of God. . ..You are of God, little children, and have overcome them, because He who is in you is greater than he who is in the world.*"

"Yahshua has authority over demons. Luke 4:35-36, NIV. "*Be quiet!" Jesus said sternly. 'Come out of him!' Then the demon threw the man down before them all and came out without injuring him. All the people were amazed and said to each other, 'What is this teaching? With authority and power, he gives orders to evil spirits and they come out!*"

"God makes demons tremble. In James 2:19, "*You believe that there is one God. You do well. Even the demons believe—and tremble!*"

"If we are true to Yahshua and obey Him by faith, we do not need to be afraid of Satan's power. In Luke 10:19,

NKJV. "*Behold, I give you the authority to trample on serpents and scorpions, and over all the power of the enemy, and nothing shall by any means hurt you.*"

"Does that clear things up?"

Carol smiled and nodded her head. The Holy Spirit had confirmed Jack's words in her spirit.

# CHAPTER EIGHT

Hiram Windsor stood at the large glass window and thought hard about the information, and the lack of support his "god" had given him. The demonic realm had suffered greatly in conflicts with this particular team of Yahveh's warriors over the last two years and was not interested in helping him fight them. It was up to him to figure out how to defeat them.

"Great! The demonic doesn't want this fight". He got the distinct impression that Satan and his legions of demons were hoping that the Albatross could eliminate the Crossfire Team for them because they had been unable to do it themselves over the last several years of battle. It was either a supreme compliment or they were throwing him to the wolves. It wasn't hard to guess which one Satan thought it was.

The only fact of any real interest the demon had given him was that he did not need to hunt down or seek out the Crossfire Team. They were coming to confront him very soon. Somehow that worried him. But, he had overcome much larger and more dangerous opponents many times. He would prepare a trap for them that would eliminate their spiritual advantage. Then he could easily defeat them. This could be a major event in his rise to ultimate power. He chuckled to himself, "These clowns are going to quickly realize they weren't as capable as Hiram Windsor." He made some calls and prepared his trap. Now, he had to arrange some terms between Satan and Yahveh so that the Crossfire Team would have to win this fight strictly in the natural.

Mark Connelly was praying for heavenly guidance concerning the upcoming action with the head of the Albatross. He prayed from his heart to Yahveh in the name of His Son, Yahshua. "Heavenly Father please guide me as I lead this battle to overcome Hiram Windsor and the Albatross today. I submit all that I am, including my training, my experience, and my abilities to You Father."

He sensed a presence and opened his eyes to see Raquel the Archangel floating in front of him with a serious look on his face. Mark said "Amen" and got off his knees. "What's up Raquel?"

Raquel studied Mark so intently it caused the former SEAL concern. The Archangel suddenly asked Mark, "If you and the team had no heavenly assistance could you still take on Albatross and win?"

Mark frowned because the question reeked of supernatural politics which always put the humans and their world on the chopping block. He frowned and asked, "Raquel, what do you classify as "heavenly assistance"?"

The Archangel looked even more serious. "Your Force Generators, your armor and swords, the Matrix, any angelic information, support, or backup, and any supernatural interference against the human enemy."

Mark smiled, "What did Satan have to give up to get a concession like this from God?"

Raquel shook his head, "He gave up the worldwide Ebola plague the demonic has been spreading. This will save thousands of lives and decrease fear everywhere. It is what the Most High has wanted for a long time."

Mark nodded his head. "It is a worthwhile deal, but to allow heaven this gift we have to accept the loss of our supernatural gifts as God's warriors and still defeat a multibillion dollar, hundred-thousand-man army with only thirty-five godly saints using only our earthly talents and capabilities?"

Mark looked at the obvious pain playing across the angel's face and smiled. "No sweat, we got this. I would ask if we can still pray even if God won't respond." He stood up and stuck his hand out. As Raquel took his hand Mark patted the angel's hand with his free hand. "I know that this tearing you up inside as our fellow warrior who has been sidelined. But, Raquel, be of good cheer because we still have all the advantages we had before we became the Crossfire Team and even if we lose, our reward is to live in Heaven with you and Yahshua forever. Don't take any bets against us. Either way, I'll see you here or on the other side."

Mark walked off to tell the rest of the team the new rules.

Raquel felt sadness and anger at the price his friends would have to pay and pride at being friends with humans who could teach angels things about bravery and faith. He would never defy the Most High, he couldn't, and it wasn't in his nature to do that. But there were things he could do within the rules that could shift the odds of the coming battle.

# CHAPTER NINE

Jack and Laura listened to Mark without comment as he explained what God was asking them to do and what they would have to do without. When he was finished Jack asked, "Raquel's first question is still the most important, can we do it? And, if so, how do we do it?"

Mark sat quietly for a long period trying to square his complete submission to God, doing things God's way rather than relying on his flawed human training, experience, and knowledge and this sudden reversal needing him to function using only those skills. True to his hard learned lessons he continued to pray and seek guidance from on high. This time there were no angels or words from God. Just a solid peace that thwarted any panic or doubt that tried to rise up to defeat him. He remembered all of the conflicts since he had learned to lean on the Lord and realized how much his capabilities had grown over the last three years.

Mark looked at two people he loved more than his own life and smiled confidently. "We are going to dazzle him with our technology and then hit him from a totally unexpected direction. His plan will fail and ours will work because we have more honest talent and skills than he does. As far as the "deal" goes that prevents us from working with, and relying on Heaven, I have learned to trust God enough that I'm pretty sure Satan will break his word to God before long and then God can get back into the game. I'm also pretty sure God knows I am expecting that to happen."

Laura laughed a small laugh and smiled at Mark. "Deal us in; I trust your judgment and your faith. So plan it like it is all up to us and keep our faith in God and count on the dishonesty of Satan."

Jack grinned at the others, "This is just like our first team efforts in Colorado and Israel. I'm all in also."

Mark thought about his sketchy plan and liked it. He called an "all team members meeting" and prayed for guidance anyway.

When everyone was present Mark stood up. "All right folks, here's the deal. Hiram Windsor is a brilliant and determined bad guy who always plans his fights to the last detail. We are going to throw his plan into disarray. Now he is a blooded warrior and will have a backup or fallback plan. I have a pretty good idea of his initial and backup plans based on his recorded history. If he has to go to a backup plan it is normally sheer power and overwhelming numbers. This has worked fairly well for him in the past. But, he has also had a significant number of losses. "

Mark brought up a drawing on the screen. He used a laser pointer to indicate where he was talking about. "Mr. Windsor knows all about us because he has studied our history. He also knows our numbers and roughly when we will attack his location because of his demonic connections. I don't know if there will be any actual demons involved but I am planning for that possibility."

Mark took a drink of water and grinned. "We can't trust Satan to keep his word but, we **can** trust him to break his word. Knowing we don't have our armor or swords or even any angelic backup I believe Satan will be eager to send in his demonic troops if he sees the Albatross losing this battle. That will be both a negative and a plus for us. I expect us to win this fight by getting Satan to violate his word to Father God at the smallest excuse because he so wants to take me out."

"So that's the basic strategy for us to do our job this time. Does anyone have any questions?"

Thirty-four hands went up as one.

Mark smiled. "Okay, Jack, let's start with you."

Jack nodded, "How do we foil Windsor's original plan?"

Mark took on a serious look at Jack. "We are going to telegraph our assault strategy to come at him from the last place he would expect us. That is where he will have his heavy hitters anyway. In reality we are going to do an explosive entry where there is no path into the building. This will have his assets out of position. As they scramble to engage us, the other half will come in where the shock troops are vacating. We should catch them in pincer envelopment and destroy them."

David was next. "I take it that in your plan, this is where the demons will be unleashed?"

Mark was nodding. "While Raquel did not say that Satan would also be bound to not interfere, this is a time when God has clearly told us several times that our armor, sword, and Force Generators would be available to us in any demonic overload situation. God does not lie and He never goes back on His word. That would be the tipping point in the battle and we can deal with Hiram Windsor then."

Sarah Connelly was a beautiful dark haired Israeli woman with extreme capabilities in the spy world and in combat. At five-foot, ten inches in height she could match any man in hand-to-hand combat or weapons. In shapely figure and attitude, she felt she and Laura were very much alike. Decisively deadlier than her best friend, her dark brown eyes were in constant motion. Years as a field agent and assassin for the Israeli Mossad made her a good match for her husband, Mark.

Sarah commandeered the next spot. "Okay, what if it there is a delay that takes some time until our swords and FGs are permitted and we face demons?"

Mark grinned, "Then keep reducing the human element and try to avoid combat with the demons if possible."

Sarah shot back, "They will be hunting us down and they are indestructible if God allowed them into our dimension!"

Mark's grin got bigger. "Then just shoot them to death."

Sarah started to shake her head and then a light shone in her eyes and she grinned back at her husband. "I like it!"

Mark spoke to everyone. "God loves us and isn't leaving us to fight totally alone. The special anti-demon ammunition bunker is full and we will be using it."

Amid great cheers and relieved laughter Mark held up his hands. When everyone had settled down he said, "Remember, this could be the actual equalizer and so, we may not get our other toys back. Also, we still have to overcome all of Albatross' soldiers to win the day. This will be a fearsome battle and we need to be on top of our ability just to survive. I have confidence in each and every one of you. I will give the sub-team leaders detailed plans on the way there. There, by the way, is northeast of London in Brittan. And one more piece of good news, we will be travelling in the Ghosts and the Formidable".

More cheers as the meeting broke up and everyone went to prepare for the battle in the dawn.

# CHAPTER TEN

The explosion was unexpected, coming as it did at 5:00 o'clock in the morning. Its force was so immense it threw Hiram Windsor out of his desk chair and slammed him against the wall of his office. He was followed immediately by his multi-million-dollar desk which pinned him against that same wall. He was unconscious so he didn't notice the desk or the fact that the blast removed fully half of the top floor of the building, including half of his office, directly across from his present resting position.

A large aircraft came to a hover next to the opening and five warriors jumped from an open hatchway into the remaining office space. It took all five to move the desk away from Windsor's body and extract him. Mark Connelly quickly checked the man's vital signs and ran a DNA test kit based on the only known DNA sample of Hiram Windsor from a battle in Israel two years earlier. Assured it was the actual leader, Mark then injected him with a sedative and a powerful time delayed muscle relaxer. Putting the unconscious Hiram Windsor into a body bag they moved him to the hole in the wall and caught a cable thrown by one of the SOG from the hatchway in the Ghost II. Hooking up the body bag to the cable they transferred the unconscious man to the aircraft which closed the    hatch and moved away quickly.

Jack was talking to the pilot of the Formidable, which was hovering one hundred yards away covering the war going on two floors below the team leaders. Jack agreed and caught Mark's attention. "You were right, we caught them totally flat footed and David and the troops have the rest of their troops bottled up defending the main access." Jack waved his arm around the damaged office. "This was interesting; I didn't see this in your plan."

Mark grinned, "Pure on-the-spot inspiration my good man". He moved over to the doorway into the building, with the others following him. "I had no hint the man's ego was this big. He was doing routine office business while waiting for us to attack him tonight as we let slip that was when we coming. But, when I saw the LandSat image of him as we approached; I just couldn't resist grabbing him."

Jack shook his head. "It was a miracle he wasn't killed by the blast or that great, huge desk of his."

Mark shrugged, "Acceptable losses, I personally didn't care if he made it or not. As it is, he should still be a real challenge for the Mossad interrogators in Tel Aviv."

Jack frowned, "The Israelis know Windsor is the head of Albatross and that he works for Marco Marino. Why are they willing to help us at such a possible price? You have to know that Satan will tell Marino where he'll be."

Mark shook his head. "Doesn't matter to them because of all the Israeli lives Windsor destroyed trying to give Israel's enemies an advantage in the Middle East. They have wanted to arrest Windsor very badly. The General told me himself *"If you ever get your hands on this man, bring him to me."* I knew it meant a lot to him."

Jack asked, "What about our task to brace him after defeating him so that God could take his demonic connection from him?"

Mark looked inside himself before he answered. "I believe we will have accomplished that by giving him    to the Israelis. Now let's go downstairs and help the others rout these leaderless vermin."

Spreading out as they approached the stairways Mark had 1/2 pound of C4 explosive taped to each of the elevator doors. If the enemy tried to come up that way and get behind them via the elevators the triggers on the C4 packages would ensure that wouldn't happen.

Just as they reached the landing above the pitched battle Jack felt a catch in his spirit. He used his battle comm and warned the entire team, "Watch out for demons, stay sharp!"

Mark changed plans and motioned everyone back from the edge of the landing. He talked on his comm to Rob in the Formidable, "On my mark take out this whole building." He switched channels on the comm and told David to withdraw as they had rehearsed earlier. Mark got his group back up the stairs and back out through what was left of Windsor's office. He got a signal from David the others were clear and running for shelter.

The Ghost I was just outside their original entry point waiting with its hatch open. Mark was the last member to leave the building. As he jumped into the plane, it rapidly flew away from the structure, Mark said "Now Rob."

Rob had timed it out so that the Formidable overflew the building at speed just as the Ghost I left. Rob dropped a "JDAM" 2000-pound bomb directly down the hole created by the earlier bomb. This time the entire building literally exploded outward in a wave of energy that reduced the building and Albatross' troops to fragments. Mark watched the destruction and then told the autonomous aircraft to land near the rest of the Crossfire Team who had found shelter nearly a half mile from the target. Mark and the command crew disembarked and joined the others as they prepared to fight the real enemy.

# CHAPTER ELEVEN

Mark knew the devil was going to throw everything he could at them because he thought they were unarmed. He had everybody trained not to focus on one target but to conserve ammo and pick individual targets that no one else was shooting. He told Ethan to give him a direction towards any rift that was opening near them.

When it started Mark realized he may have somewhat underestimated the devil's bet. It seemed the enemy was going "all in" as six rifts opened around the 35-member Crossfire Team. Mark spoke on the communication network, "Plan C ladies and gentlemen"; this aligned five or six members of the team toward each rift.

In a synchronized attack, demons flooded out of all six rifts at the same time. There were demons of all sizes and any description that could be called evil, ugly, and threatening. To an uninitiated person all these walking, loping, or crawling creatures would have struck raw terror and immobilizing fear in their hearts and minds. To the well-seasoned members of the Crossfire Team they were nothing but evil that needed to be removed by any means available.

Mark had everyone hold their fire until the leading demons were fifty feet away and then ordered "Fire!"

The bullets with the esteem of Yahveh on their tip instantly killed the physical bodies of any demon they touched. The demon hit would quickly dissipate into demon stain that covered those demons behind it.

The first ten minutes of withering fire reduced the ranks of demons to the new ones exiting the six rifts.

Suddenly, all the rifts disappeared and silence fell on the battlefield. Standing next to Mark, Sarah shook her head, "I've got a bad feeling about this."

Mark was about to reply when ten larger rifts opened all around the team members. Hundreds of demons roared out of the multiple rifts to attack the humans. Even with everyone firing it was obvious that the remaining demons would swarm over them in a few minutes. No one broke and ran regardless of their impending doom.

As the warriors cut down the ranks of the oncoming demons, the newest tier of demons reached hand-to-hand combat range. The most proficient of the swords people let their rifles fall on their slings and drew their Katana, Wakizashi, or Tanto swords and attacked the closest demons.

Mark had explained before they left their ship that at this stage of the battle the demons would be here illegally and could be maimed and killed with a normal human powered sword. True the demons would be more powerful than us but probably just as stupid and inept as usual. Beware that without God's power; just striking a demon will not kill it. A sword had to deliver a true killing strike to disable or kill the demon.

They knew the odds but each man or woman stood bravely to do battle with Satan's hordes. The advantage for the team members was Mark's strategy. As a swords person engaged a demon and set it up, one of the armed troops would shoot it while it was stopped. There were injuries and bashing that would leave bruises for a time but because of their skill with the sword the team had prevented any deaths that day.

Mark and Sarah were dueling with four demons at once. It wasn't the same four demons continually because David, Laura, and Megan continued to shoot the ones in combat with the couple. The dead demons were replaced immediately every time. Mark realized Satan had put a bounty on his head because he really didn't like Mark.

Two more demons tried to get at Mark at the same time and the battling was fierce. Mark knew at the rate he and Sarah were tiring it wouldn't be long before they missed a defensive move and that would be that for them.

Suddenly there were heavy explosions at each of the rift openings that blasted demons to bits by the hundreds as the Formidable joined the war. This reduced the number of demons to a more manageable number for the team but their supplies of ammunition were running low     at this point.

Sarah waved and then shouted to Mark over the noise of the battle. "I thought that bombs couldn't kill demons legally in our dimension."

Mark yelled back, "That's true, but we dispatched a lot of them earlier. I doubt that old sparky got permission for this lot." He switched magazines to load normal ammunition and shot three more demons which blew holes through them and they dissipated. "That's what I thought!"

Mark called Rob in the Formidable. "Hey Rob! These demons are here illegally, shoot them all."

# CHAPTER TWELVE

The Formidable proceeded to use its six chain guns to kill every demon on the ground and then used ten mini-drones to take 2,000 pound charges into each of the rifts and detonated them. This closed all but three of the rifts and no demons came out of those after that. Eventually those rifts snapped closed and the Formidable quit firing and began to act strange and dip and spin over a wide area. It finally settled down and returned to its station-keeping position above the team.

Mark called the plane, "Hey Rob, got problems?"

Rob answered, "Nothing my friend and I couldn't handle."

Mark was about to respond when Raquel appeared before him grinning widely. "Mark, you've done it again. Satan couldn't overcome your defense with the Most High's ammunition and in his all-consuming anger Satan violated the terms of his agreement with God by introducing hordes of illegal demons. Your spirited defensive effort stymied him again. At that point God told him to stop attacking you and the team. You now have the angels and your "tools" back." In a flash the Archangel disappeared.

Mark told the troops that their armor, swords, and the force generators were back on line. He called both Ghost aircraft to land and load troops for a return to the Sword. He had Jack, Laura, and Sarah join him to return with Rob on the Formidable.

As they were walking to a suitable landing place, Rob called and warned him about an approaching military vehicle.

Eyeing the approaching APC, he said to the others, "Looks friendly but switch on your FGs just in case."

Jack asked, "Who are they?"

Mark said, "I'd guess they would be the UKSF, The United Kingdom Special Forces group. It is a directorate of the UK Ministry of Defense. UKSF is commanded by Director Special Forces, usually a SAS Major-General who is higher than a Brigadier who is over both the Special Air

Service or SAS and the Special Boat Service or SBS. This looks to be a Colonel in F Company, Royal Marines, of their "Tier 1" special forces. Tier 1 due to fact they are the units usually tasked with direct action."

Mark saluted the Colonel, "Good afternoon Colonel. General Mark Connolly, Crossfire Team, I expect you're here about our little dust up with the Albatross Empire and their friends."

The Colonel returned the salute. "John Grimes here, yes, we were assigned to investigate what the neighbors here called a small war. We stopped by the crater that was the site of a battle. Your handiwork I presume?"

Mark nodded, "We made sure the conflict didn't spread beyond that one building."

The Colonel didn't seem happy. "Well, the problem here is that there doesn't seem to be any authorization for this action on British soil. Therefore, I am supposed to take you all prisoner and inter you until the government determines what to do with you."

Mark smiled a small tight smile, "Colonel, did you see the battle going on here until just recently?"

The Colonel made a grimace, "Yes, though I am not sure I can believe what my eyes saw."

Mark nodded, "Those were demons from hell. That is who we fight against for all mankind. Those "things" are under the control of Satan, the enemy of God and mankind. The government of the United Kingdom has ceded control of your country to Marco Marino who also gets his marching orders from Satan. We serve Yahveh God and don't answer to any government. The Albatross is the military arm of Marco Marino's little one world government. The creator of the universe told us to capture Hiram Windsor and demolish his organization. That is what we have just done. You know God is doing the heavy lifting on this one because we have done all this with thirty-five men and women. We just defeated over one hundred of Albatross' best soldiers in a hardened site which was operating in your country committing crimes around the world, and probably over a thousand of Satan's demons. So, I respectfully suggest you go back to your Major-General and tell him we declined your invitation."

The Colonel shook his head, "I'm afraid not, General Connelly. Look around you. I have over two hundred SAS troops and ten tanks facing the four of you. I demand your surrender!"

Mark casually checked the Force Generator's LED and found it glowing green. Clicking on his comm he asked, "Rob, you've been listening to this, can you handle it?"

Rob came back with, "You bet I can! How about a demonstration?"

Mark stared into the Colonel's eyes as he shrugged his shoulders, "Sure, try not to kill any of our SAS friends if you can help it."

With a gut-shaking deep vibration the Formidable appeared directly over the team members and one-by- one all ten of the British heavy tanks were lifted by their front ends and rolled slowly over onto their tops.

Mark looked at the Colonel. "You now have 200 SAS warriors and no tanks. Suddenly there were yells and screams from all directions. Mark and the Colonel looked around at the British troops who were all throwing their rifles to the ground. "Now you have 200 unarmed men surrounding us. I'm sorry Colonel; we need to be leaving now."

The four team members started to walk away when the Colonel pulled his pistol and shot at Mark six times. Mark waved goodbye to the man as the field from the force generator stopped the bullets in flight leaving the Colonel baffled and upset.

The Formidable landed and the team members boarded. The plane rose off the ground with such a deep vibration the SAS soldiers were covering their ears and doubling over.

Jack said, "I would expect a visit from the RAF soon."

Rob turned toward the Atlantic Ocean and accelerated to Mach 4, "I doubt that. I don't believe they have any fighters that can even do Mach 3."

Mark looked at the flight deck floor and said, "Rob I think we need to talk."

# CHAPTER THIRTEEN

Rob sighed, "Yeah, I agree. As you can see some demons came to call on me. I knew what you told your people about their vulnerability to regular gunfire. But, I won't kid you, those things scared me half to death, I could see their evil intent in their eyes. They had come here to kill me. I pulled my service pistol and shot three of them before the gun ran dry. At the same time, I was trying to keep the plane in the air. I hit the station keeping autopilot and grabbed for a magazine as I dumped the empty one but realized I would not have time before they got to me. Plus, there were more of them coming out of a tear in the inter-dimensional wall on the plane. That's when your friend Raquel showed up and went Cuisinart on them. In no time at all, the entire rift closed and there were no demons left, just their mess." Rob indicated the copious amount of demon stain on the floor and the bulkheads.

Mark prayed silently and received a leading. "Rob, I believe God is telling me to have you seconded to the Crossfire Team and get you trained in spiritual combat. How would you feel about that?"

Rob smiled, "That's what Raquel said you would say. Anyway, I've had some time to consider and pray about it. Although I'm thirty-five unlike the majority of your team, I'm willing to give it my best. I really didn't like those creatures trying to kill me. Heck, you guys pay half my salary right now anyway. Let's just make it happen before I change my mind, okay?"

Mark nodded and reached out to shake Rob's hand. After landing on the Sword and securing the Formidable in the below deck hanger for refitting and refueling, Rob and Mark went to Rob's superior officer. After explaining Rob's introduction to demonic warfare he was approved for reassignment and training.

Mark turned Rob over to David for housing and the grand tour. Sarah set up a training schedule and evaluation series for their newest member.

Jack called Mark to the War Room. As Mark walked in Jack looked up at him and shook his head. "Hiram Windsor attempted to escape from the Mossad Interrogation Unit two hours ago. He was tased six times and he still didn't give up."

Mark nodded, "That sounds like the man, were there any causalities? "

Jack nodded, "One dead and three injured. He is holed up in a sealed ward with three more hostages. He is apparently aware that he is not going to escape alive and he has demanded that you and I meet with him as we are the only people in the world that he will negotiate with. Since then he hasn't spoken a word. The Mossad Director says we dumped him on them and she expects us to straighten things out. She also said to bring Laura and Sarah with us."

Mark surprised himself when he suggested they pray for guidance. He sat down just as their wives walked into the War Room. Jack gave them a quick update and they all bowed their heads in prayer.

Laura had that out of body feeling and opened her eyes to find the four of them in a beautiful heavenly setting near a calm river and resting in a great peace. As they sat there on the grass a feeling of great harmony and satisfaction swept over them and Laura was led to stand up and walk into the water which she did. She sensed the other three people walking with her. Laura felt led to continue walking into the beautiful water as the bottom continued downward. She knew God was in control and didn't hesitate as the water closed over her head. She had no problem breathing under the water and kept walking forward. About twenty feet further the bottom leveled out and Laura sat down and relaxed.

Hours went by and she felt refreshed in her mind, body, and noted her spirit was singing psalms of praise and thanks to the Father in a continuous litany of love.

Sometime later she got up and left the water feeling completely refreshed and at peace with everything. Jack put his arms around her and hugged her gently. She had never experienced such complete harmony with him as she did then. The four of them sat down together on the grass and waited. Raquel appeared and greeted them.

"From the Most High God, Peace to you and welcome. Yahshua wanted you to have this time as a freshening." Raquel turned and went to one knee with his head bowed as the Savior walked up to them. The four team members knelt alongside of Raquel in humble obedience to their Lord and King.

Yahshua sat down with them. *This meeting with Hiram Windsor is critical to Israel, the team, and especially to Windsor himself. He is asking for you not to seek an advantage for him but, through you, to find salvation in my name. He will become a powerful force for good and against the anti-Christ."*

*"Don't be surprised by this. He is probably the most terribly lost soul since Saul of Tarsus in my time on Earth. Like Saul he has led forces against my people and committed many sins in doing so. Also like Paul he will serve me with complete obedience and finally in love for my people. His service will more than atone for his sins but will become a great example for millions of the lost throughout and after the tribulations."*

*"Our Father in heaven has forever blocked any demonic contact for Hiram Windsor so that he can serve with no reservations. Because of that sudden loss of evil guidance, he is truly lost. Go in my Name and offer him the gospel in truth and love. I will see that your mission is successful in the eyes of the people of Earth and the heavenly host."*

The Lord faded away and the team members and Raquel found themselves in the War Room on the Sword.

Raquel's eyes blazed like the sun. "I am so honored to have been with you at this time. The rebirth and new life of Hiram Windsor will be a great milestone in the course of God's chosen people on Earth. Interestingly, an angel could not bring the gospel to this man. As earthly warriors he will trust you but he will always be wary of spiritual beings after dealing with Satan."

Raquel stood tall and smiled, "I salute all of you." He then disappeared.

# CHAPTER FOURTEEN

The small "Fragment" UAV from the Sword landed at Sde Dov Airport which includes an Israeli Military air base ten minutes outside of Tel Aviv. Jack, Laura, Mark, and Sarah were driven to the Mossad Headquarters building and met Director Jakobson outside the sealed ward where Windsor was confined.

Jack explained to Iris Jakobson what they had been told by the Savior concerning Windsor and his future.

Iris sighed heavily. "Every member of the Mossad and especially the Kidon wants this man dead many times over. Most of these people do not believe in Yahshua and will not listen to even you whom they greatly respect in this matter. I doubt that they will even obey me if I ask them to spare his life."

Mark was praying silently when a plan appeared in his mind. "Director, I may have been given a solution to this impasse. The Savior's plan will succeed regardless what anybody does but this concept could prevent any bad feelings in the future."

Knowing Mark's penchant for impossible plan executions the Director smiled, "Tell me."

Mark gave a brief outline of the operation and then asked for a chance to speak to Hiram Walker privately.

Iris shook her head. "By our rules I must have at least one member of the Mossad in attendance when anyone except the Mossad is interfacing with a prisoner."

Mark nodded his head and waited until one of the Kidon surrendered his weapons and accompanied him into the sealed room.

Even though he hadn't eaten in several days Hiram was alert and poised to explode into action at any second. He stepped forward and motioned the other three people in the room to leave. This was his agreement if the Crossfire Team came to talk to him. When the three men were alone Mark asked, "Why did you ask to see us?"

Windsor evaluated Mark and found his spirit to be far more imposing in person than his previous view of the man on video. "Originally, I wanted to kill you myself, but now I want you to tell me what to do. Never in my life have I lost my confidence or control as I have now. But, I have a sense that you, somehow, are going to guide me to my destiny. Is it even possible *you* do that?"

Although this was delivered in a snobbish, superior tone and attitude Mark wasn't flustered in the slightest. He looked the criminal mastermind directly in the eyes and said, "You need Jesus."

This statement caused Hiram Windsor to back up a step and the Kidon agent to snort in derision. Windsor looked at Mark and realized he was serious. "You know me and the records of all the crimes and atrocities for which I'm wanted, why would God want anything to do with me?"

Mark smiled, "Because you were meant for greater things, which is why Satan derailed you into the life you have led. God knows your true potential and you need faith in His Son and His redeeming grace to reach your true potential. Let me ask you this, look into your heart and tell me if you still feel seething anger and consuming hate for all men?

Windsor stood there for several minutes. Then, with a look of astonishment he said, "No, I only feel sadness at the things I have done and the lives I have destroyed. I don't sense Satan anymore."

Mark nodded, "Then repeat after me." The dreaded Hiram Walker fell to his knees and repeated the words after Mark as tears ran down his face. "Dear God in heaven, I come to you in the name of Jesus. I confess to You that I am a sinner, and I am sorry for my sins and the life that I have lived; I need your forgiveness. I believe that your only begotten Son, Jesus Christ, shed His precious blood on the cross at Calvary and died for my sins, and I am now willing to turn from my sin."

"Right now I confess Jesus as the Lord of my life and my soul. With all my heart, I truly believe that your Holy Spirit raised Jesus from the dead. Today I accept Jesus Christ as my personal Savior and according to Your Word, right now I am saved."

"I thank you Jesus, for your unlimited grace which has saved me from my sins. I thank you Jesus that your grace that never leads to license, but rather it always leads to repentance. Therefore, Lord Jesus, transform my life so that I may bring glory and honor to you alone and not to myself."

"I thank you Lord Jesus, for shedding your blood in seven different places to restore me in this life and for dying for me at Calvary and giving me eternal life."

"Amen."

Mark helped him to his feet and hugged him. The Kidon agent was shaking his head. He looked at Hiram Windsor and almost shouted, "This phony little play of sorrow and false conversion is not going to save you. I person..."

The agent's words ran out as he saw his first demon. It appeared behind Windsor and ran a large black sword through him from the back so hard it came out the front covered in blood. Hiram Windsor screamed and collapsed to the floor.

Mark's armor and sword burst into glaring life as Mark prayed and confronted the demon. As they fought, two more demons appeared and one went for the Kidon agent and the other joined the attack on Mark. Twice, the Kidon agent evaded the sword of the demon attacking him but was quickly running out of room. Another flash of white light announced the arrival of Raquel the Archangel. All three demons tried to flee only to find the Angel Caleb standing between them and the rift they came through. The rift snapped shut suddenly and the battle was over in seconds as the demons evaporated into demon stain.

Caleb picked up the body of Windsor and vanished. Raquel looked sternly at the Kidon agent. In his deep Bass voice, he gently said, "Release your anger or it will soon control you. It opens a door in the supernatural which gives the enemy access to your life. Repent of your anger and unforgiveness so that G-d can forgive you."

Looking at Mark, whose armor and sword had faded away at the demise of the demons; he said "You have done God's will. Although Hiram Windsor is no more, you did save him." Raquel faded out of sight.

The two men went out of the sealed room and met with Director Jacobson. The agent reported that Hiram Windsor was killed by a demon and an angel took his body away. Mark agreed with the man's story and ruefully said, I believe this concludes the reason for our being here."

Laura shook her head, "Not until we have dinner with Iris and bring her up to date on our progress since we left Israel."

After dinner Iris looked at Mark, "I know the official record of the demise of Hiram Windsor; now tell me what really happened."

Mark smiled, "The real story is that Hiram Windsor really did die in that room. He will never come back and he is doomed to be forgotten quickly." He looked his friend Iris for a minute. But, Robert "Bob" Vance was reborn there at the same time. That was the real name of the man who became known as Hiram Windsor. Bob had no more than accepted Jesus into his heart when this demon appeared and tried to skewer Bob through the back with its sword. Raquel was there but not so we could see him. He deflected the sword thrust and "imagined" the blade coming out the front covered in blood. Bob's scream was genuine but "urged" out of him by Raquel."

Seeing the look on several faces he smiled, "Don't worry "Bob" was unconscious before the demon attempted to kill him. That's why he collapsed so realistically. The Angel Caleb then picked him up and took him to David Zahavy on the Sword. That was the end of Hiram Windsor in this dimension and since the Kidon saw him killed by the demon that resolves the Israeli righteous anger problem."

Iris nodded her head. "I see; therefore, I would not be lying when I say that the criminal mastermind known as Hiram Windsor was terminated during imprisonment by a demonic agent?"

Mark agreed, "You would be telling the truth." The team left the Director and returned to the Sword. On the flight Laura asked Mark, "I read in the records that Hiram Windsor was of Arabic background, why was his name "Bob Vance" rather than an Arabic name?"

Jack smiled, "Raquel told me that Hiram was deliberately misled by Satan to increase his supposed "anger" against the world by being of Muslim descent. The only Arab relationship in his history was distant cousin who was not even in Hiram's bloodline."

Laura agreed with him. "So, will we be interfacing with "Bob Vance" on the Sword?"

Mark shook his head, "No we won't. Bob is already in route to the United States for his introduction to his new life and calling. Yahshua will have him in intense training for fourteen months and then he will begin to walk out his original calling."

Jack nodded his head. "That would leave just enough time for Bob Vance to become a household name in both the Christian and Jewish worlds before the mid-point of the tribulations."

Laura smiled, "I see, with God as his marketing agent unheard of Bob Vance will become well known in the right circles as an anointed man of God."

# CHAPTER FIFTEEN

The next morning the entire core team met in the War Room on the Sword.

Mark brought everyone up to date on the resolution to Hiram Windsor and Bob Vance.

Jack and Laura had spent the evening and part of the night in prayer concerning their next moves against the Albatross Empire. Jack spoke up after Mark's review was completed. "We have accomplished our task of cutting the head off of the snake with the Albatross Empire. Now we have been tasked with eliminating twelve of their most violent projects. Eight of these projects have demonic elements which would have required our attention anyway. The loss of the leader doesn't affect these projects until they are completed. The other sixty-four Albatross projects are falling apart without leadership involvement."

Jack threw a chart up onto the main screen for all to see. "These are the twelve projects the Crossfire Team is to terminate. I've assigned one of us to lead one or two SOG members depending on the forces involved. All of us are swordsmen or women and three or four team members should suffice according to Mark's critical assessments."

"As one team succeeds they will become available to lend support as needed by the others. There is a schedule on this chart for each of you to get with Mark as to the particulars of your assignments and advice as to how to start. Laura and I are going to pray for all members' success before we start moving out after lunch. We're going to share transportation so plan on multiple groups being assigned to each aircraft. Also, two members of the core team are not leading a group. Ethan is simply too valuable of an asset in his job as ComSec Manager for all of us. He will stay on the Sword and support us all at the same time. In a sense he will be a remote member of each team. Remember, there is only one of him for everyone to share, play nice."

Jack looked at their newest Core Team member. "Christi, you are still too new at combat to lead a team. I'm going to assign you to Sarah's team in lieu of one SOG member. Learn from Sarah and the way she does things because your turn to lead is coming soon."

"Let's break for now and everyone prepare for your missions, I'll see you back here at 1 p.m. for prayer. God strengthen each of you."

Jack and Laura spent their time together praying for heavenly angels to guard each of the team members and asking Yahshua to cover them all in His atoning blood that He shed in seven places at Calvary.

At 1 o'clock in the afternoon the two of them prayed for everyone and saw most of the others off before they had to part for their own missions.

At 2 o'clock Sarah, Christi, and Molly Grant from the SOG left on the Ghost I for a small island in the South Pacific Ocean. Sarah outlined their destination, their target, and the probable course of action.

Sarah smiled at the two young women who were acting somewhat subdued to be going into action without any backup or their Force Generators. The Father had not authorized the ultimate defense devices as they would provide such an unfair advantage to the Team members that it would violate God's concept of balance between forces. Only if the enemy confronted the team with overwhelming odds would the Force Generators function to balance the odds.

Sarah displayed a map she had on her large tablet screen. "As you can see, the island which we are headed for is largely uninhabited. The large resort on this island is normally crowded by three hundred guests. The entire complex has been taken over by the WSO which is a World Security Organization not controlled by Marco Marino. They are meeting for an urgent conference on emerging terror threats. Attendees to this conference come from every first tier country in the world. They are the best at what they do and even with Marco Marino trying to disband them; the multi-national group has eliminated twenty-four terroristic groups in the last year."

"We know this forty person strike group of the Albatross is being tasked to disrupt their conference but we don't know how. I propose we find their team and select someone who might know what is going on and ask them."

Christi exchanged looks with Molly. They were both aware of what "Ask them" meant.

Christi asked Sarah, "How do we find the Albatross people? After all, we have no official standing unless the fact we're on the Anti-Christ's bad list means something."

Molly shook her head, "We might even be on the WSO's bad list. Do we have to avoid and evade them while we're trying to keep them safe?" Sarah laughed, "Molly, you've got the wrong attitude. We are on God's side and He and His Angels fight for us and stand alongside of us."

"The WSO had bettered hope they are not on OUR bad list. I think the Albatross Empire already knows they are on our naughty list. But, you guys have given me an idea. Let's pray and ask Yahshua to convince the WSO we're the good guys and have them arrange a meeting with us to work together."

The three women bowed their heads and prayed fervently for God's assistance and guidance in this matter. Sarah felt a presence and opened her eyes to see Raquel the Archangel sitting with them. The golden eyes of the Angel studied Sarah and he nodded his head and then faded from sight. Sarah could see that both of the other women were also aware of Raquel and his answer.

# CHAPTER SIXTEEN

Sarah keyed her comm unit and spoke to their aircraft. "Land at the resort airfield in full view of the people there."

The computer on the plane acknowledged her command and changed their flight path. As they approached the airfield they received an open air radio message. "Crossfire Team, please land at our field and taxi to the large hanger with a blue band near the north end of the terminal. We will have ground transportation waiting for you. Welcome to the conference."

Sarah acknowledged their request. She looked up and smiled. "Okay ladies, business casual dress and weapons."

After landing and deplaning they were driven to the resort's main building. Getting out of the cart they entered the building and were greeted by the leader of the WSO, Former Chairman of the U.S. Joint Chiefs of Staff, General Howard Miles. Sarah grinned and shook his hand, "Hello again General Miles, it will be nice to work with you."

The General smiled and greeted the three women warmly and had them sit down with him at a table in the lobby. "It's nice to see you again so soon, Sarah. I assume your presence here means that we have a serious problem that we are unaware of, right?" Sarah nodded and explained their assignment to him. He listened intently and then asked, "Why only the three of you? Didn't you just say that the assault team from the Albatross numbered forty?

Sarah agreed, "Yes Sir. But the entire team is responding to twelve different groups simultaneously so we're spread a little thin. Rather like the old adage, "One riot, one Ranger. Mark evaluated the odds and felt we would be sufficient to resolve the problem after praying about it. I asked God to synch us up with the WSO so that we wouldn't step on any toes. I honestly had no idea you were involved."

The General grinned, "Just like old times, right? Well, this is a top notch group but I'm glad God has assigned you three to help us. I'm going to have the head of our internal security, Major Edward Smythe work with you directly. He's ex-SAS and a dedicated soldier. I'll bring him up to speed on your operation. I have so many irons in the fire at this conference I can't give you the close cooperation you need. Ed will be able to do that. Just in case you need me, here's my phone number. Anything urgent, you call me. Understand?"

The General excused himself and walked away. He came back ten minutes later with a slender man with a shock of red fuzz for hair and a blue-eyed British face. Ed Smythe was a no nonsense officer but he sported an easy smile and a happy-go-lucky earnestness to came across as friendliness. After General Miles left, the Major asked Sarah about any information they already possessed concerning the assault on the conference.

Sarah filled him in on what they knew and explained her idea on getting the information. The Major thought for a moment, "Right on, if you don't mind I'd like to tag along on your fact-finding operation. I always like to learn from the best. And, from what General Miles explained to me about your team, I'm ready to go to class."

Sarah agreed with the Major and asked him where he stood concerning God, Jesus, and religion.

The Major looked somewhat distressed or possibly dismayed by the question, "What difference does that make?"

Sarah smiled to remove any sting from her next comments. "Because, the Crossfire Team works for and with God to accomplish His goals and plans. You need to understand that our operations frequently involve supernatural events and players."

Ed Smythe looked like he might have bitten into something rancid. "What do you mean by "supernatural players"?"

Sarah looked the man directly in the eyes, "Angels, demons, and things like that."

Having been given a stern warning about the lethal capabilities of Sarah and her teammates, the Major was careful in answering. "Oh, I see. Never seen either of those yet."

Sarah grinned slightly, "Stick with us Major and you probably will get a chance. You didn't answer my question though and it could be important."

The Major nodded, "I go to an Anglican church and have sworn my life to Jesus. I pray frequently and believe in the resurrection of the dead." Sarah nodded, "Good Man Major, you're definitely heading in the right direction. Please join us in a short prayer to determine our first steps in information gathering."

Sarah led the four of them in prayer to uncover the Albatross team. "Father God, show us how to get the information we need to do your will in this matter. We thank you and ask this in your Son's name Jesus Christ."

As she stopped speaking she saw a series of visions detailing where the Albatross team was and a man who would be their target. Ed Smythe was stunned; he had also seen the visions.

Thinking carefully, he spoke up, "I know where that building is here on the island."

# CHAPTER SEVENTEEN

Positioned on a hillside overlooking the suspect building the team observed the two-story, supposedly abandoned place. It looked deserted if you didn't know what to look for. Major Smythe and the three Crossfire Teammates knew exactly what to look for.

For example; the windows covered with tarp material too new to have been on the building when it was abandoned. The many new footprints leading into the front door which hadn't been swept away. The flash of movement at several windows indicated inhabitation and most telling, the thermal scope that indicated more than three dozen heat-producing bodies inside the building.

The Major looked at Sarah, "I believe you have found the buggers. Now, how do you select one that knows the score? Praying again?"

Sarah shook her head, "No, what we do is; watch the deep thermal scope and find the active ones; those would be the non-commissioned officers. They know it all and run it all too." She used the scope and pointed out two of the images of that type. She smiled, "Now all we have to do is to watch until one of these either leaves the building or goes to the lower floor to do something."

An hour and a half later darkness had fallen when she called attention to one of their selected shapes who was headed down toward the first floor. "Let's move now before he goes back up."

As the four-person team ran carefully down the rest of their hill and closed with the building while staying to cover as best they could, the Major looked at Molly, "Why would he come down to a supposedly empty floor?"

Molly grinned. "He's taking a potty break of course. Since they don't have running water upstairs, they've probably built a gravity feed toilet on floor one, away from their living area for privacy and odor control."

The four flattened against the wall of the building as Sarah used hand signs that Christi and Molly cover her and the Major as they "borrowed" their target for a short talk.

Sliding through a crumpled doorway Sarah got over to the make shift toilet area just as the user stepped out, zipping up his trousers. Stepping lightly behind him Sarah jammed a stun gun against the back of the man's neck, triggering the 50,000-volt unit as it contacted skin. The man stiffened and his eyes rolled up until only the whites showed. Sarah and the Major caught the man as he collapsed and carried him out of the building through the crumpled doorway. The group quickly moved away from the building with Christi and Molly sweeping the footprints away with the leaves on a couple of small branches they had found on the ground nearby.

Two hundred yards away from the building the Major and Christi kept watch. Sarah and Molly injected the man with a truth agent and slowly brought him to a state of heightened awareness. Then they questioned the hostage for ten minutes before rendering him unconscious again. Pouring some cheap rot-gut whiskey that Sarah had intentionally brought with them, down his throat and spilling some of it on his shirt they removed any sign of the interrogation. Then the Major and Sarah quickly carried him back to the building and left him with the bottle in his hand outside the crumpled door. Racing back to their vantage point, they waited until two security guard types found him mumbling and sipping on the booze. They pulled him inside, none too gently.

The team moved over the hill and stopped in a small secluded valley to sum up their findings. Sarah looked grim as she spoke to Major Smythe. "These thugs are planning to kill or capture everyone at the conference. They've already planted enough explosives to destroy all of the main buildings at the resort. Whoever survives the explosions will be captured and tortured until they give up all their contacts and plans for the war against the Albatross. Then they will all be killed."

Sarah stared at the Major. "What are you able to do to prevent this mass slaughter?"

The ex-SAS officer nodded, "Quite a bit actually." He took out his cell phone and called his group's military communications officer. "Rodney? Major Smythe here, I'm requesting an emergency Evac of all personnel in the next forty minutes. Use plan Alpha Three. I want everyone off the island by 10 hundred hours with the exception of the sixty man flying squad who I want to my coordinates in the next two hours. Move it man, this is critical!"

He then called another number and waited for a response.

Meanwhile Sarah used the card General Miles had given her to call him. He answered immediately. Sarah could hear an alarm sounding in the background as she brought him up to date on their discoveries. He thanked her and told her that the attendees to the conference were already leaving the island with practiced skill and almost military coordination. "I'm glad you gave us an edge on this Albatross group. Thanks, gotta go, talk to you later."

Sarah was about to tell Major Smythe the news when Christi caught her attention. Christi bent down and whispered to her. "That remote camera you had me leave watching the Albatross hideout is showing a coordinated exit of the Albatross team. They loaded onto two large trucks and tore out of there. I think they are headed to the resort."

Sarah hit redial but got no answer from General Miles phone. Sarah quietly told Christi and Molly, "Watch out for a possible double cross by Major Smythe or people on his team."

Sarah dialed another number and said three words "Find me fast."

The three women moved apart and quietly surrounded the Major. Sarah asked, "How are things going at the resort?"

The Major looked puzzled and said, "Something's wrong! I've lost contact with my number two. I need to get to the resort immediately." He ran over to the four- wheel drive vehicle they had used to get there and jumped in. He fired up the engine and waved the women to hurry and join him. Sarah yelled, "You go, we'll find our own way back."

The man shook his head and spun the wheel to the left and tore out of the valley. As the sound of his departure faded out, the quiet sound of the Ghost I was heard as it landed behind them and opened its hatch.

After boarding, Sarah put a call into Ethan Reaper and explained their situation. "I am not sure about the WSO security apart from General Miles. His head of security,

Major Smythe, worked with us on our info raid but I'm not sure if he's been turned or if he just didn't realize his group had been infiltrated and apparently neutralized. He's headed back in a 4-wheel drive to the resort. If you can put eyes on him see what happens when he gets back."

Ethan asked, "Are you guys safe? Where do you want the Ghost to land?"

Sarah didn't have any answers to those questions. "I think our first order of business is to find where General Miles is and make sure he is safe. We could also use his input on his group."

Christi waved her hand at Sarah and leaned in toward her, "We can track General Miles, I put a tracker on him when we met him today. You know, just in case."

Sarah smiled, "Oh, you are one smart girl, aren't you?"

Christi smiled and gave Sarah the tracker number. Sarah entered it into her tablet. It immediately located the tracker unit. It was at the Main building of the resort. Sarah called Ethan and had him connect her tablet to the eyes on effort.

The Starlight optics on the Ghost showed several of the Albatross soldiers dragging an unconscious Major Smythe out of the darkness into the well-lighted building. Sarah could see blood running from a head wound on the limp form. Sarah shook her head, "Well, it looks like the Major and the General are both prisoners and if our information was correct then they have extremely short futures." Molly racked a fresh round into her M8. "Then I suggest we go get them back before they become unimportant to those thugs."

Sarah scanned the single story main building and counted twelve moving heat signatures on the thermal scan. There were five unmoving heat signatures, three of these were fading out. The three women geared up and had the Ghost drop them off two hundred yards up the seaside beach. The Ghost then moved off and flew into the area in front of the main building. Anyone that fired on the plane died in a hail of minigun rounds. Sarah led the other two women into the building through the seaside doors. They immediately kicked their way into the room with the fixed heat signatures.

The attack by the Ghost was having its desired effect drawing most of the Albatross soldiers to the front of the house. As she entered the "interrogation" room with her M8 up and searching for targets she encountered a man holding General Miles in front of himself with a gun pointed at the General's head. Sarah calmly put a round through the man's head followed by two more as the now-freed General dove for the floor.

Christi took out two more soldiers before they could fire their weapons. Molly took out one and drew down on the last enemy soldier who dropped his rifle and raised his hands saying "I surrender". Molly said, "I accept your surrender" as she put four rounds through the man's chest killing him instantly.

Sarah had released the General's bonds and he took one of the unfired weapons from a dead man's hands. He said "thanks" to all three women. Then, as Sarah checked on the Major he looked at Molly. "Normally, honorable soldiers don't kill people who give up their arms and surrender."

Molly smiled, "As would I, except he was already going for a hideout pistol. So, he wasn't really unarmed, was he?"

The General walked over and saw the pistol in the dead man's right hand. He looked at Molly, "I ask your forgiveness for my comment. You were right to shoot the rat."

Sarah got a groggy Major Smythe up and moving. She had seen Christi checking the other two men and a woman. Christi shook her head; they were beyond saving in this world.

Sarah led the group out the seaside doors and back down the beach. She signaled the Ghost which was still trading shots with a mounting number of Albatross fighters in the building. The ship fired two hellfire missiles which blasted the whole building to splinters. Then it flew down and landed between the team and any possible survivors. The five people boarded the plane which then lifted off and moved several miles away from the island.

Sarah told Ethan that the Major's "Plan Alpha 3" managed to get most of the conference members away safely before the Albatross descended on the rest of them. General Miles had fought with them but was captured along with Major Smythe. "They were supposed to make a video confessing their "crimes" against Marco Marino before they were beheaded."

Sarah continued, "The rest of the Albatross fighters died in a firefight with Marco Marino's flying squads which were also dispatched to get evidence of the WSO's crimes but, instead they caught the Albatross people looting the resort and attacked them."

Sarah asked Ethan, "I think we're done here so we're available to support any of the other teams. What do you have?"

Ethan said, "Hold one for Jack."

Jack came on the line, "Hi Sarah, Ethan says you and your team are available. Is everyone fit and ready for more fun?"

Sarah laughed, "Yes we're well and uninjured. We were able to save Howard Miles, again."

Jack chuckled, "I'm glad you were able to assist the General. I am going to reroute you guys to Mexico to give Alexis a hand. She's run into a buzz saw down there and could use additional support."

Sarah agreed and signed off. After dropping the General and the Major at the resort airfield and watching them fly off the island, they headed to Mexico.

# CHAPTER EIGHTEEN

Alexis dropped down behind a low stone wall to avoid the flurry of bullets seeking her life. Jon Cannon and Craig Steele were twenty feet away trading shots with six of the Albatross soldiers but equally bogged down.

Alexis Zahavy was a blonde American beauty with brains and thorough combat skills. She was five foot ten inches tall with a slender figure and blue eyes. She had just recently married David Zahavy and had a background that included years with the U.S. Army Rangers and four years with the U.S. Clandestine Service. After several parallel operations with the Crossfire Team she had asked to be reassigned.

Alexis thought back on how they got into this mess.

--------------------------\*\*\*\*\*\*--------------------------

Their assignment was to stop an assassination that was supposed to remove an opposition candidate who was running on an anti-Marco Marino platform. The Albatross was tasked by Marino to remove the candidate in a manner that no one will defy him again. To Alexis that meant explosions and big ones. She and her two SOG soldiers had determined where the attack would take place and scouted the area under darkness and found all the Semitex locations. This hadn't been too hard since they were all wired together. They deactivated the triggers on the charges and rerouted the wires so that everything looked good but no explosions.

That had been all well and good but when the charges didn't blow the Albatross decided to use brute force and charge the meeting in an attempt to apparently gun the candidate down.

Alexis and the two SOG members intercepted the Albatross charge and were cutting the twelve-member hit team down when their reserves showed up. Now there were over twenty new fighters and three of the original group trying to kill the three Crossfire team members.

Moving from their defensive position to break off the battle they had been caught between forces when the Albatross split their forces and used a low ridge to leapfrog half of their team and get ahead of the three-person force that had spoiled their operation.

------------------------\*\*\*\*\*\*------------------------

Alexis came back to the moment as new rounds impacted the ground near her opposite the side where the rocks were protecting her. The crossfire team hadn't planned on a protracted fire fight and their ammo was quickly running low.

There was an ominous vibration approaching their position and Alexis realized that as close as they were to losing this battle the addition of heavy artillery or an armored vehicle would finish them off. Suddenly four of the Albatross troops charged their position and first Craig and then Jon jumped up and counter-charged the attackers, firing as they went. Alexis saw them both get hit by rifle fire several times and Jon went down. Alexis jumped up and ran toward the enemy firing her M8 as fast as she could. She knocked down the last enemy standing as Craig stabbed his K-Bar knife into his opponent, ending his life. Two rifle rounds hit Alexis' body in the back and slammed her off her feet and into the ground.

Lying on the ground in pain she heard more small arms fire and felt more than heard rounds whispering by her. She then heard the sound of several chain guns clattering out death and she waited for it. But, it didn't come near and she forced herself to one knee and started to cry as she saw the Ghost aircraft chewing up the remaining Albatross fighters. It only took seconds. She struggled to her feet and stumbled over to where Jon lay on his back. Craig was keeping watch over him with his big bloody knife. She heard Sarah call her name as she felt for Jon's pulse. There wasn't one and then she turned Jon's head to her right and saw that he had taken a fatal head wound behind his right ear. She shook her head at Craig and tried to rise. That didn't go very good until Sarah and Christi took her arms and helped her to stand.

Sarah helped her to the Ghost and got her inside and back to the small area behind the seats and onto a gurney. She gritted her teeth and said, "I'll be alright. Get Craig in here. I saw him get hit several times in that last defense."

Craig was putting a body bag with Jon's body in it in the storage area next to the gurney, "No thanks, I only got hit on my armor, no penetration."

Sarah had been struggling with and finally got Alexis' body armor off and expertly inspected her damage. Finishing her scan, she smiled, "Well, young lady, you are still dancing between the blades. Your armor also stopped the two rounds that hit you. It's going to hurt like sin for a while but you'll live."

Craig shook his head, "Jon took a round that cut his helmet strap and then, just as the helmet flew off his head he got hit just behind his ear from the front. I doubt that he even knew what killed him." Tears ran from many eyes as Craig continued, "He's with Yahshua now. But I'm going to miss him for a while."

# CHAPTER NINETEEN

Sarah put a call in to Ethan for another assignment only to learn that all the assignments had been completed and the teams were all being called back to the Sword.

Half-way back to the ship Jack called Sarah. "Sarah, I need your team and Alexis' team to resolve one more Albatross assignment. I know you've had two battles already but you are the only team available to take on this job in time. It was a deep cover assignment that we just found out about that is far more important than all the rest we tackled. This mission will definitely include demonic forces and is to stop a demonic thrust aimed at the heart of Israel. I would use our entire Team but the timing is critically short and everyone else including Mark and myself are scattered right now. Are you up for this?"

Sarah laughed, "Jack the island job was basically a smash-and-grab and Alexis had just about finished up the job in Mexico. We do have Jon's body with us and no refrigeration available so that could present a sanitation problem."

Jack prayed for a bit and told her, "I will have the Ghost drop you guys off and bring Jon back to the Sword. At the same time, I'll send a second ship with additional team members to support you. It'll be the first team that makes it back to the ship to refit and rearm. I'm sending the assignment parameters to your tablet. You can also add Ethan Reaper to your team as you'll be the only group working. Let me talk to Alexis please."

Sarah handed her phone to Alexis. She talked for a few minutes and then hung up. She handed the phone back to Sarah. "Craig and I are seconded to your team spy-lady."

Sarah smiled at the Mark's pet name for her. "If I get tired I may let you run things. You're quite capable you know. Now huddle up with me while we study this new Albatross wrinkle that Jack has bestowed on us."

The new job was a human and demonic attack on the higher Rabbis in Israel. Especially on the person of Rabbi Ben Chanan. This effort was designed to defame and or destroy the rabbinical leadership of Israel. Sarah called Ethan and asked what he could add to the information.

Ethan sighed, "I've tried everything I can think of but the people in the Rabbi's office keep assuring me that the Rabbis are safe and they have everything under control.

Sarah thought for a few seconds. "Ethan, see if you have satellite coverage of the area around Rabbi Chanan's offices and look for any demonic activity. Since he lives there you'll be covering his residence too."

Ethan said, "Hold one." A few minutes later he came back on line. "No sign of demonic activity at present. But, you know how quickly that can change."

Sarah agreed, "Keep a watch over us when get there in twenty minutes. Our presence could spark activity."

Ethan laughed, "Not to worry, I've got a lock on you right now. You should eat that apple you've got rather than just tossing it in the air."

Sarah frowned, "That's awfully tight satellite coverage Ethan. How are you doing that?" Ethan laughed again, "When Crayton locked onto you after you called he also activated two screen shots from internal cameras inside the Ghost. Don't fret about it, your privacy is secure. Even Crayton knows when to break coverage. I'll be watching for bad guys, Ethan out."

Sarah grinned remembering when the three-woman squad changed clothes prior to their island arrival. She debated telling them about the coverage and decided it would serve no purpose at this point. Next time would be different and she'd warn them about the camera coverage.

Sarah told everyone on board, "Pack up everything, we're sending Jon back in the Ghost to the Sword."

Alexis got a call from the Mossad Director. Iris Jakobson had been asked by Jack to support Sarah and the others in their effort to derail this latest Albatross action.

Thirty minutes later the four women and Craig watched the Ghost fly away. Craig flagged down a Mossad vehicle that was coming to pick them up and they loaded everything and everyone into the large SUV.

Arriving at the large building the team disembarked from the SUV. As Sarah and Alexis went up to knock on the door. The door was slammed open from the inside, and two men came out roughly pushing a Rabbi ahead of them. The

Rabbi stumbled and fell to the walk and cried out from pain when his shoulder struck the ground. One of the two men shoved the Rabbi with his foot and yelled at him in Hebrew.

Sarah was irritated by the crude behavior and yelled in Hebrew at the two men to leave the fallen Rabbi alone. Both men turned their attention to Sarah and walked toward her with menace in their eyes. Sarah set her jaw and met them halfway. The first man tried to grab her hands but only grabbed air. Sarah side-stepped that man and closed with the second man who was pulling a pistol out from under his coat.

Using her left hand, she grabbed the pistol and rotated it to her left disarming the man and incidentally breaking two of the man's fingers. He yelped and Sarah used a palm heel strike to his chest with her right hand using her forward momentum knocked him backward to the ground. Rotating to her left she swung the pistol and knocked the first man out cold. She stepped back and reversed the pistol to cover the man on the ground.

Holding his broken right hand with his left he said, "You are going to prison for assaulting two federal officers!"

Sarah stepped up to the man and knelt down next to him and shoved the pistol under his chin. "So, it won't cost me any more for killing you?"

The fear flared in his eyes and he said, "Please don't kill me."

In Hebrew Sarah said, "First, Israel doesn't have Federal Officers and second, if they did, they wouldn't act like the two of you. Now tell me who you are and who you represent before I pull this trigger!"

The man blurted out, "We're officials of the Albatross Empire and we represent Marco Marino's One World Government. You are in a lot more trouble than you realize. I ..."

He lost his voice when Sarah shoved the barrel of the pistol deeper into his throat. "Why were you abusing this Rabbi?"

"We were assigned to bring him into our headquarters. We can do whatever we want to detainees. No one has the authority to stop us."

Sarah smiled, "Oh yeah? Well I stopped you!" She reversed the pistol and slammed it against the man's head hard enough to knock him unconscious.

Craig and Alexis had helped the Rabbi up and cut the plastic cuffs off his wrists. Alexis asked him if he was all right in Hebrew.

He nodded his head and thanked Sarah for saving him. He didn't understand what was going on and just wanted to go back into the building.

Sarah told Craig to bind both men and keep a watch on them. She accompanied the Rabbi back into the building and went with him to the office of Rabbi Ben Chanan. The young Rabbi knocked on the doorpost and was granted permission to enter. He kissed his fingers in reverent awe of Yahveh God protecting the entrance and touched the Mezuzah on the doorpost.

The Rabbi explained all that had happened and Sarah's rescue and then bowed and left the office. Rabbi Chanan got up from behind his desk and came around and took Sarah's hand. He thanked her for her assistance and asked how it happened that she was there.

Sarah explained the Crossfire Team assignments from Yahveh to stop the Albatross attacks around the world. Then she told him of her assignment to save the Rabbinical structure of Israel from the combined Albatross and demonic forces arrayed against them.

Rabbi Chanan thought and prayed about this. Finally, he declared G-d's protection had been sufficient for several thousand years and would still take care of them in these present circumstances.

Sarah looked at the most powerful Teacher in the nation of Israel and suggested they pray together to resolve the apparent contradiction in the Most High's requests and assurances in this matter. The Rabbi agreed and they got on their knees and prayed for clarification.

There was a bright light added to the office and they both looked up to see the Archangel Raquel standing before them. Sarah smiled and said, "Hello again Raquel, mighty warrior of the Most High. Do you bring us an answer from Heaven?"

The golden eyes of the Angel focused on Sarah. "I do, now hear the word of the Most High. *"My children, know this, the Earthly servant of Satan, Marco Marino, wants to destroy the Rabbinical culture of My chosen land of Israel and is using an attack by agents of the Albatross Empire. Satan is eager to ensure this destruction and will use his demons to spread fear through the Rabbinical hierarchy. This must not be allowed to happen! I have commanded My servants of the Crossfire Team to prevent this atrocity. Rabbi Ben Chanan, Satan is seeking your life and wants to mislead you. Heaven protects you but he has gained legal access to you through an old forgotten sin of pride. Repent and I will forgive this sin forever. Petition Me and I will fight for you."*

The Rabbi confessed and repented of his sin and sought forgiveness immediately. Then he asked for G-d's help with these attacks. He looked at Sarah, "Again I must say, I am so blessed when I am with members of your team. I have read the writings of a thousand rabbis from the beginning of the rabbis until now and not one, I repeat, not one, has ever spent time with an Angel let alone an Archangel as I have been honored to do."

Sarah smiled, "Tell me Rabbi, and how were you able to accept the visit from Yahshua, the true Son of Yahveh God considering the normal rabbinical stand that He was not the Messiah?"

Rabbi Ben Chanan coughed, "Well, even rabbis can be wrong every now and then."

Alexis made a face, "True, but for two Thousand years? What have the other rabbis said when you told them that you met Him yourself?"

Rabbi Chanan laughed, "Oh, I haven't told them yet. They are a hard headed bunch, as was I, and would not accept my story as truth. Don't look so concerned. Yahshua told me not to speak of it yet. Very soon everyone in Israel will be shown the truth. I was blessed a little early, that is all.

# CHAPTER TWENTY

After Sarah and Alexis left Rabbi Ben Chanan, the five team members went to an empty classroom in the building to plan their next steps. Craig had surrendered the two Albatross thugs to the Mossad and joined the others.

Sarah led a prayer for direction and protection. No answers, no angels, only a sense of urgency. Sarah's cell phone rang. Rabbi Chanan was shrill with overtones of fear and he spoke rapidly, "There are demons in the school here. Please save the students!"

Sarah took off running out of the classroom as she told the others of the call. Craig pointed down a side hall where teenaged males were dashing away from one classroom down the hall. Sarah pointed at Christi and Craig and that classroom as screams came out of a closer room. This room she pointed at Alexis and Molly. She ran to the middle room by herself.

As Craig led Christi into the first room they found a six-foot tall, black as night, demon holding the teacher on the floor and keeping five young men corralled in a corner. As Craig charged across the floor the demon turned toward him and raised a black sword. Craig started praying his battle prayer and his silver armor and shield suddenly appeared along with the chrome sword with the essence of Yahveh flowing off of it. Craig's face showed the Holy anger of God as he rushed the demon; who at this point was back pedaling to keep space between itself and Craig.

Two more demons came out of a small rift and vectored toward Craig, raising their swords. Christi's golden armor flashed into existence as she began to pray and she cut down the first demon with a single overhead stroke. The second demon turned to battle Christi leaving Craig free to hack the first demon to death which he did with great fervor.

Christi was able to defect the second demon's ebony sword with her glowing sword and ran her blade up the demon's arm and through its neck, killing it instantly.

In the closer room Alexis watched as a particularly ugly and deformed demon killed a young man with a sword thrust through the man's chest. Eight other young men screamed or covered their eyes to avoid looking at the horror facing them.

Alexis and Molly both started praying and their armor and swords exploded into sight as they closed with the demon. The demon tried to flee to the rift it had come from only to find the Angel Rose clothed in her bright white power energy with the wrath of God on her face. The demon charged the Angel but Rose stood her ground and with a single mighty stroke of her sword she cleaved the Demon from its head to its stomach.

Suddenly eight or nine more demons exited the rift and set to attacking the Angel and the two women in gold armor. Molly pushed the switch on her body armor and was rewarded with a green LED indicating that her Force Generator was working. Molly touched her Com switch and said, "Force Generators are working! Molly out."

Sara heard Molly's call as she entered the middle classroom and switched on her force generator and started praying at the same time. There were nine or ten demons in that room and they all started to attack her at the same time. The demons could not understand why the woman was smiling against such odds. Less than fifteen minutes later the last of forty demons died also wondering why his sword hadn't hurt her at all.

The five team members met back in the hallway after ensuring the safety in the classrooms. After listening to the other two reports Sarah frowned. "We are missing something. These skirmishes are not the reason we are here. They are little stage plays meant to keep us occupied while the real effort is something else." She put a call in to her husband, Mark.

Sarah explained her feelings about things and asked for his advice.

Mark prayed and then responded, "I think you're right spylady. That amount of action can't be the major thrust. "He added, "Hold on for a few minutes, please."

Sarah grinned when she saw Mark loping down the hall with David Zahavy and Ethan Reaper. She hugged Mark and Alexis did the same with her husband, David. Sarah asked Mark, "So, you turned out to be the first ones back to the Sword?"

Mark nodded, he took Sarah's hand and they went back into the empty classroom she had just been battling in. Mark noted the massive amount of demon stain on the floor and just about every other surface. He looked at Sarah, "How many demons did you terminate in here?"

Sarah thought and grimaced, "About thirty-eight or forty, mostly small ones, a couple of big ones, and nine sleek ones whose skill could have been a challenge if I hadn't had the Force Generator."

Ethan had been watching his tablet, "Zero demonic activity for now." Mark nodded, "Check with Carol and ask her what the matrix shows for the next twenty-four hours in Israel that would concern us."

Ethan nodded and set to work on his computer tablet.

After talking to Carol he looked up at Mark, "The news isn't good. Satan has requested permission from Yahveh God for human dimension travel for over eighty thousand demons with bodies. Ninety percent of these are requested for the area of Israel. That's seventy-two thousand demons! The requested "first wave" starts three days from now."

Mark nodded his head, "Okay, thanks Ethan. Have Carol keep me up to date with the seventy-two thousand demon attack."

Ethan smiled at Mark, " Will do, Boss."

Mark and Sarah knelt together and prayed for God's guidance for His warriors on the battle lines with this immense horde of demons. Even with the Force Generators it would be impossible for thirty-five men and women to stop this flood. Mark had tears in his eyes as he prayed. "Father, that would mean each person on the team would be facing at least two thousand and seventy plus demons here legally if you allow it. And we both know that Satan is a liar and he will bring in twice that number of illegal demons." He took a deep breath and shuddered.

Then Mark relaxed and he smiled as he declared, "I know that You have everything under control and I am not worried about the final outcome. Regardless of the outcome we will fight the fight You have called us to fight. I know that each and every man and woman will do their absolute best for as long as we can. Thank you Father for this opportunity."

# CHAPTER TWENTY-ONE

Carol continued to watch the matrix for any indication of change in the massive request by Satan for God's permission to enter eighty thousand demons into the human dimension. The request remained unchanged for the next two days and Carol was distressed to the point of fear. Fear for all humanity as well as the Crossfire Team. She knew in her heart and soul that Yahveh was a good God that loved all His children but this would be a total massacre on an unimaginable scale. Finally, she reached her breaking point and asked God to release her from her duties and let her join her friends and fellow warriors in the physical defense of the people of Earth.

During this very heartfelt plea her mind and soul were filled with peace that was like a tidal wave breaking over her and totally washing away all tightness in her gut, all fear or concern for the team or the people of Earth. It was a watershed event in her faith that eliminated any worries or cares. She felt the loving arms of Yahshua surround her as she thrilled to the response to her prayer.

The voice of the Messiah was filled with love for her and God's children. *"Carol, do not fear for your friends or the people of the Earth. As you believe, our Father in Heaven will not allow the destruction of the race by Satan and his demons. At no time has, or will, God grant Satan this request. In fact, it was because of your role as an observer of the event matrix that the devil made such an extreme request. As usual, this was a lie to throw you and the team into fear and confusion. The Father allowed this to happen to mature you in your service to his warriors. Your fear was generated by your true knowledge of the Father's love against this apparent disastrous event. It does you honor that in the extremity of this confusion that you thought only of your friends and my sheep. Learn from this that your faith in the Father is, was, and always will be true. Now see that the request has been denied and removed from the matrix. Take this good news to the team."*

Carol transitioned back to her room in the ship and suddenly found three people around her. Jack, Laura, and Ethan were soggy and dripping wet and holding a sheet over her. She realized that she was also totally soaked with water running down her to splash on the floor. She exclaimed, "What happened?"

Laura laughed, "It seems that we, unfortunately, totally under-estimated the amount of light and heat those diamonds of yours could create. Ethan alerted us to the fact that the fire alarm sprinklers were going off in your room. We overrode the entry protection to find the sprinklers going full tilt trying to extinguish your heavenly indicators. We had just shut them off when you came back. Welcome home."

Shaking her head to get the water out of her ears Carol laughed with the others as they tried to dry off. Then she remembered her mission. "Hey guys, good news! The Father denied Satan's request to bring thousands of demons into our dimension.

"Jack smiled, "I guess I can truly say, Thank God!" Carol shook her head sadly, "I'm afraid it was all an effort to use me to mislead you all. Yahshua said the Father allowed it to stay to "mature" me in my faith. I'm sorry."

Jack could sense the truth of Carol's statements. "Don't feel bad, it was a maturing process of the faith for all of us. Everyone realized that this might be the Earthly end for them and came to the understanding that our futures are secure in God regardless of anything. I, myself stopped worrying when I realized the whole problem was above my pay grade and I knew that God had everything in His hands and under His control. It wasn't just a lesson for you, young lady. Be at peace."

Ethan looked at his, thankfully, waterproof tablet and smiled, "Let's find some towels and grab some clothes for Carol. We need to move out of here to let the maintenance people get in here to restore the room. I've notified the team and told them the good news." Ethan grinned, "I think I heard a huge collective sigh of relief."

They left and went back to their apartments to dry off and get redressed. Laura took Carol under her wing, "You can clean up here and you can stay at our place tonight. Anyway, I have to apologize for your recent baptism in your room. God gave me a small vision of you while I was praying for you today. It showed you swimming while dressed. I couldn't figure out what that meant, Sorry."

Carol smiled, "I'm just glad you were there to keep my head above the water."

Thirty minutes later Mark called Jack, "I appreciate Ethan's good news but the battle goes on. We need a Core Team meeting in the next hour if possible."

Jack agreed and called the meeting.

When everyone was present at their positions Jack gave the floor to Mark. Mark presented a map of Northern Israel on the main screen. "This represents a potential demonic attack site as determined by information from Rabbi Ben Chanan and his office. The rationale is that this is a critical meeting of the rabbinate with selected leaders of the evangelical churches from the United States, Europe, and the Far East. The rabbis are praying for support from these churches beyond the financial assistance they are already providing Israel. Instead of money they need concentrated prayer support to fight against the enemies of Israel."

"When the Rapture occurred a great deal of the Christian support were people who went to heaven in the Rapture. This support helped greatly by praying to God for his protection of Israel and seeing Him move against the forces of evil in this nation. Miracles abound when God moves and the loss of international prayer support has resulted in a noticeable decrease in these miracles since the Rapture. I agree that this will be a prime target for Satan to bring demons into our dimension since the people attending are fairly immune to normal demonic attacks."

"I want inputs as to what each of you think these attacks will attempt to do and when they might occur. I would also be interested in your ideas of how we can protect the conference attendees."

"I will let you know whatever Carol finds on the matrix as soon as we insulate her fire sprinkler system from her praying place."

This resulted in a great deal of laughter which broke the serious mood of the meeting.

# CHAPTER TWENTY-TWO

The site of the interfaith conference was at the Churchill Auditorium, Technion, located in the city of Haifa in Northern Israel. The conference was to start on Monday at seven a.m. The Crossfire Team was provided housing in a nearby Mossad facility since they arrived early Sunday afternoon. After visiting the Auditorium and conferring with Rabbi Chanan they mapped out their strategy with the assigned teams of the Haifa Police, the Mossad, and the IDF.

Meeting back at the Mossad enclave Jack poised the critical question for their defense to Mark.

"Well, now we've seen the auditorium what is your opinion on how will they attack? And, will this just be a scare tactic or an actual attack?"

Mark thought back to the conversation he'd just had with Carol Moffet when they landed in Haifa.

----------------------\*\*\*\*\*\*----------------------

"What did the matrix show you about this event?"

Carol was much more confident after her short period of uncertainty and heavenly intervention. "Well Mark, the matrix shows a request to allow entry for forty demons at this site tomorrow morning. The request has been granted, but, we both know that the devil is a liar and he'll bring at least twice that many illegal demons. He is able to do that despite God's restrictions on any further entry of illegal demons because nobody knows how many illegal demons he already has in our dimension that he can use." She looked seriously at Mark, "Also there is something unique about the forty legal demons. I don't know what it is except that they will be different than our usual, run-of-the-mill demons."

----------------------\*\*\*\*\*\*----------------------

Mark looked at his best friend and shook his head.

"The best professional guess I can give you is that I believe that this will be an all-out attack to kill all of the attendees and completely squash this international support for Israel. I see them flooding this place to overwhelm us while other demons do the killing. Carol also thinks the forty legal demons are unusual or unique and different from normal demons. This may be our sternest test to date. I know we'll have our Force Generators but that won't help the other people here if we're too busy to save them."

Jack nodded his head, "Yeah, I agree with you Mark. I've been getting a bad gut feeling about this coming battle ever since we were assigned to it by God. Well, let's get the best advice we can." He looked up, "Raquel!"

The Archangel appeared in his jeans and denim shirt motif. "How can I help you Jack?"

Jack smiled, "You would help me greatly by telling me about the demonic assault and what we're up against in this attack by the demons in the morning."

Raquel shrugged his shoulders. "As your intelligence people say, "I haven't been read into this action as yet." I'm sorry Jack, but the Most High believes that you and the rest of your team can handle Satan's fallen angels and appears not to be worried about the upcoming battle. Rest assured that I and the other angels will be close by and are ready if you need help." He waved at Mark and faded out of sight.

Jack sighed and shook his head. "I must be getting spooked. If Raquel says the Father doesn't seem concerned, then maybe we're over-thinking the problem."

Mark looked at Jack, "Let's prepare for the worse anyway. It can't hurt to be over prepared."

Jack agreed because his spirit wasn't settled after talking to Raquel.

They made a trip to the armory and made sure all troops were issued a full load of the special ammunition and grenades with the esteem of Yahveh glowing on the bullet tips and packed into the grenades. Jack called a special prayer session where Mark explained what he thought was coming and coached everyone on how to fight beyond their limitations. Jack prayed for the entire fighting team and individually for those that requested prayer.

Later, when Mark was doing paperwork at a desk in the Mossad housing, Sarah sat down next to him and quietly asked him, "Is it really going to be as bad as you described in the meeting?"

Mark tried to never lie, especially to his wife and he knew the best way to prepare her for the morning was to tell her the truth as he felt it would be. "Yeah I think so. It'll be a tough battle and there could be casualties on our side this time. We really need to warn the attendees about the impending attack." He was irritated and somewhat upset by what he believed the morning would bring and that Heaven didn't seem worried about it. Sarah put a gentle hand over his bigger hand and smiled. "So? We've faced tough odds before and won through. We're very good at what we do, let's trust the Father and do our best."

Mark realized she was right. He sent a mental prayer to Yahshua and gave his worry to Him. "You're right Spy Lady, like Jack said, "This thing is significantly over my pay grade anyway."

Mark called Rabbi Chanan and strongly advised him about the attack and the fact that the conference attendees should have the opportunity to leave before the attack. The Rabbi advised against it and possibly driving off the people permanently when there was a real possibility that it was just a ruse to derail the meeting. "We've had similar alerts before and wasted several meetings and nothing occurred. I will admit that up until now we've never had warnings from the Crossfire Team and I've seen with my own eyes your capabilities. Isn't there a reasonable likelihood that the demons won't want to do battle with your team?"

Mark laughed, "Rabbi, you could be right. I'll tell you what. As the conference opens, give Jack ten minutes to give the attendees a heads-up advisory as to what to do in the event there is an attack. These are seasoned warriors of Christ that love Yahshua and they probably won't cut and run anyway. You remain on the platform and assure them of the situation as you see fit, okay?"

The Rabbi agreed and hung up.

Mark and Sarah continued to pray and seek guidance from heaven about the upcoming battle that Mark was even more sure was coming now.

# CHAPTER TWENTY-THREE

Jack mingled quietly with the attendees to the conference and greeted some that he knew. He made his way over to the stairs to the platform as Rabbi Chanan called the meeting to order and everyone sought their seats. The Rabbi welcomed the one hundred and eight attendees on behalf of Israel. He made his opening remarks and looked at Jack and motioned him up to the speaker's microphone. "I am pleased to introduce Jack Malone of the Crossfire Team. His team is here as an additional layering of protection for the conference. Listen carefully to his comments and do not scoff or doubt the truth of what he is about to reveal to you. I personally have been in his company when Satan's agents were sent to kill myself and two other rabbis and can honestly say that if he and his team had not been there to defend us, none of us would be alive today." "Go ahead Jack."

Jack was the President of his own company and evidenced a command presence with a powerful speaking voice. He was very competent on his subject and knew how to speak to others so that they would listen and learn. "Ladies and gentlemen of the international community. I will take only a few minutes of your time and I need you to understand what I'm about to tell you is not to frighten you or scare you. The Crossfire team has been anointed by Yahveh God to defend His children from Satan and his demons. Regardless of your previous experience or knowledge I assure you that demons exist and hate you and the Light of Christ that you carry. Satan is panicking as the time draws close for the return of the Son of God and His thousand-year reign on Earth. Satan is sending his demons into this human dimension with physical bodies to steal, kill, and destroy everything that is of God. Unfortunately, that includes each and every one of you. There is a strong possibility that Satan hates your support of Israel so much that he will launch an attack on this enterprise. Remember that demons are fallen angels and are much stronger than humans."

Jack could see that he had their undivided attention. Not a sound was made as they listened intently. "As I said, Yahveh God has anointed my team and eleven other teams around the globe to do battle with these demons and we are here to protect you in the event of such an attack. Do not attempt to enter into combat with these creatures if you have the opportunity. You will lose your life and endanger others around you. If an attack happens move quickly to a safer place that one of our team will indicate. As the Priest for our team I am going to pray for your protection by God and His Angels in the event of an attack. Stay in prayer and please pray for us as your defenders."

Jack looked at the silent audience. He bowed his head and closed his eyes. "Father, I pray Your ultimate protection for each and every person here from the enemies of God and mankind. Father, fill them with Your strength and peace. Fill them with Your joy and sustain them with Your love and Your peace. Father Yahveh grant us the victory over Satan and his demons. I pray this in Yahshua's name and by the blood He shed in seven places. Amen"

Jack looked up and said, "Thank you and may God bless you." Jack turned and shook Rabbi Chanan's hand. He then walked down the stairs from the podium. Everyone started talking and a solid, tough-looking Pastor from Bedford, Texas stepped up and shook Jack's hand. "I really appreciate your advice. One question though, how will we know who members of your team are? You know, to lead us to safety?"

Jack liked this man of God who walked and shook hands like a street fighter. He smiled at him as he looked at his nametag. "Don't worry about that Larry, just look for the Silver or Gold armor and a chrome sword with the power of God flowing off of the blade, that'll be one of us."

Jack stepped back into the open area near the platform and walked quickly around the bunting-draped stage and out the back door to check on the preparations to defend these people.

As he headed back to the large van that served as their mobile control center he met Raquel. The Archangel was in his fearsome Angel attire and his golden eyes looked like flames. "Jack! Thirty minutes until the assault! Satan's minions are massing to transit a rift into the auditorium east of the platform. Prepare now!"

Jack stared back, "Thanks Raquel, we are ready."

Jack turned around to find the university President and his wife standing there with their mouths open. The man swallowed and said as a matter of fact, "You weren't pulling our legs were you?"

Jack shook his head, "No, I wasn't. Please move away from this area, now!"

Jack immediately forgot about them as he ran back to the auditorium. He spoke into his combat microphone,

"All team members, attack in the auditorium in less than thirty minutes. Everyone to your places. Malone out." As he entered the auditorium, he saw Rabbi Chanan urging the attendees to walk slowly and carefully to the exits. Obviously Raquel gave him the word and he was acting on it.

As he raced past the people exiting the auditorium he saw Pastor Larry and others back near the east exit, but instead of running away they were on their knees praying for the team as Jack had asked them to do. Jack thought, "Good men and women of God." He keyed his microphone again, "David, Alexis, keep a watch on the small group praying by the east exit so that the demons don't get too close, okay?"

He got two affirmatives.

Laura caught up with him. "I've checked the team positioning and everyone is ready. Jack checked the time. "We've got less than ten minutes to go." He turned and hugged Laura, "I love you." He kissed her passionately as she kissed him back. She stepped back and smiled.

"You'd better love me buster, I've got your back."

They talked briefly and Jack felt the atmosphere become charged. They turned toward the area to the left of the platform and started to pray their earnest, from the heart combat prayers.

Jack checked and made sure both of their Force Generator indicators glowed green. Suddenly both of their armors and swords flashed into sight as a large rift opened between the demonic realm and the human dimension.

# CHAPTER TWENTY-FOUR

Demons began to pour out of the rift and look for targets of opportunity. There were almost no people there except the ones that had armor and swords. So the demons headed for the team members. With a slam of noise automatic rifle fire started shredding the ranks of illegal demons as the esteem of God on the bullets destroyed every demon they struck. Still more and more demons exited the rift only to be struck down The flood of demons continued to swell until there were so many that some were able to reach the swordsmen and women and major battles were fought claw to hand, eye-to-eye. Still the glowing warriors were able to cut down the hordes.

Ethan Reaper broadcast a warning. "Okay kids; keep an eye on the sky. We've got winged demons coming down on us from above!" He cut two demons in half with one swing of his sword. He saw a demon diving toward one of the SOG warriors when suddenly it was cut down in the air by the Angel Caleb. All at once there were a dozen Angels fighting with the airborne demons. Dozens of more demons were attempting to attack him when an explosion near the rift hurled decomposing demon bodies everywhere. A heavy machinegun opened up raking dozens of demons every second. The battle turned against the demons and the warriors were energized to higher efforts which definitely put the demons on the defensive. Even more demons flooded out of the rift to replace those destroyed. The tide of battle began to swing back to the side of the demons as the human defenders were tiring. Jack couldn't believe the number of demons being thrown against them. The number had to be close to six hundred monsters. He saw how he was slowing down in battle and he prayed for God's help. All at once there were eighty more swords coming against the demons.

Jack realized that two of the other teams like theirs had been translated into the battle. In only minutes the demons stopped coming out of the rift as dozens attempted to go back into it but were unable to get back in. They died quickly until there were none left alive. The battle was over and the other teams saluted them as they faded out of sight.

Mark was so tired he had trouble walking over to Jack. The fatigue on his face was a tangible thing. Jack noticed that their armor hadn't disappeared. He looked at Mark with the question on his face. Mark tipped his head to the right. Then Jack saw that the rift was still open.

Sighing deeply, he stood up straight and called out to Raquel.

Raquel appeared still in his awesome Angelic motif. Jack pointed at the empty but still visible rift. "What does that mean?"

Raquel frowned and mentally left to confer with God. He returned after several minutes and stared at Jack. "The Most High says that He is keeping it open because He has unfinished business with the demonic region there." The Archangel sighed just like a human being. I have a message for you from the Most High. I am reluctant to speak it but I am incapable of avoiding my responsibility in this matter."

Mark spoke up, "That doesn't sound good." Raquel stood straighter," Now hear the Word of the Most High", *"Satan has, yet again, ignored My Ordinances and My Commandments with this blasphemous attack on My children. He has done it to his own detriment this time. I will extract such a high price from him that he will never do anything like this again. I will have a single member of the Crossfire Team deliver this message to him because he will see that your team is now more important to me than he is. He will be humbled or he will be destroyed! Use this portal to locate him and deliver my message. Be brave and do not fear, I will be with you."*

Jack was stunned and yet so tired he almost couldn't get excited about this new development. He looked at Mark who just shook his head in frustration because he didn't feel strong enough to walk over to the rift let alone walk into the demonic realm on God's business.

Raquel understood their heart's desire to do God's will even as spent as they were. He also knew who God had in mind to accomplish His will. "The Most High has already selected the least experienced of the team to accomplish

His will in this matter. The anointing to be His messenger has been given to Christi Steele."

Jack and Mark both wanted to ask God to change his selection but each man knew it wouldn't matter how much they tried to change it because God had already made His choice.

Christi smiled bravely as she walked past the two leaders and over to the flickering rift between dimensions. Jack tried to go with her but wasn't able to move. He could tell that Mark was equally frozen.

Christi's armor and sword flared brighter as she stepped into the rift which then snapped closed behind her.

# CHAPTER TWENTY-FIVE

The visibility dropped from the brightness of the auditorium to a dimness centered in the red spectrum as Christi moved into the demonic realm. Still, she could see well enough to move down a corridor littered with pieces of something covered in demon stain. She realized that God was with her in every way. She was proud of herself for stepping up when He called her.

She stepped up her pace as she came out of the corridor into a vast open area. There were many demons doing obscure things everywhere and some of them noticed her. She thought, "Well, duh. Everything and everyone in here is about as colorless and drab as can be. While I, on the other hand, am lit up like a Technicolor advertisement in glorious gold and chrome."

She came around a curve and came face-to-face with a huge demon with its big black sword and a sour look on what served as a face. The demon's voice thundered, "Foolish human female, I shall have my way with you before I tear you limb from limb and eat your heart!" It stepped forward with a heavy tread that shook everything including Christi. It reached out a giant hand to knock her sword away. Christi shook her head slightly. "You've obviously been listening to your own press far too much big ugly. That is no way to talk to a lady." Christi jumped forward and quickly swung her sword in a figure eight movement that started at the demon's left shoulder, down across its body, back across its legs, back up across its torso again, and finally across its throat.

She stepped back quickly as the demon disassembled completely. Demon stain went everywhere as the creature's legs, arms, and head fell away from its body and huge gouts of black smoke blew outward from its cuts. Christi stepped over the dissipating body and continued to walk toward the middle of the cavernous space. She had done exactly the same thing to many other demons before and it didn't really delay her in her pursuit of Satan.

Several large black arrows slammed into the FG field and fell to the ground. Christi stopped and looked up at a group of demons on a rise in the ground. She stuck her sword into the ground and picked up her M-8 from its sling position. She snap-aimed as Sarah had shown her and pulled the trigger on the underslung grenade launcher. The orb shot from the launcher muzzle and arced up and over coming down in the center of the attacking group of demons.

The grenade exploded with a bright flash of Holy Fire that killed all of those demons and several dozens more within its range. Christi was starting to fill up with the Holy Anger of God at this point and decided to shortcut this process. She dropped the rifle back on its sling, picked up her sword and used both hands to drive the blade into the ground at her feet as she spoke a heavenly power word as loudly as possible.

Christi was riding the crest of the anger filling her up and she shouted, "Satan! Yahveh God calls you to account for your defiance, NOW!"

When the power word left her lips it instantly became an immense, unstoppable power that radiated outward from Christi in all directions. Every demon it touched dissolved into fragments, as did anything created, built, or used by the demonic powers. Hills collapsed, buildings exploded as God's power spread like electricity from one place to another destroying everything in its path.

When it had completely cleared a one-mile-wide circle it suddenly ceased. Christi stood resolute in the center of the circle with her hands on the hilt of her sword and waited.

With a great crash of thunder, accompanied by several lightning bolts, Satan appeared in front of the woman in the golden armor and demanded that she stop interfering in his domain. He was violently angry and held out a staff which emitted a tremendous blast of energy directly at Christi. The Field Generator absorbed the energy as if it was a mild breeze. The devil screamed curses, threats, and insults at the golden image in front of him.

Christi ignored the curses and threats and spoke one word, "SILENCE!"

The staff crumbled into dust and Satan, that old snake, was bound in cords of light which he could not break no matter how hard he tried.

Christi opened her mouth but it wasn't her speaking directly to the fearsome Lord of the Air. *"Enough! I have tolerated your defiance for too long. I am God and I commanded you to never again send physically bodied demons into the human dimension without my permission. You not only sent eight hundred of them without permission you laughed because you knew in your heart that I would forgive you and you could get away with this evil with impunity."*

*There was a moment of total silence with Satan frozen in position but listening with fear evident on his face. "But, you were mistaken in your heart and your thoughts. I have prepared your replacement who can fulfill all prophesy and all righteousness without directly defying me. But I am not without compassion even in your case. I have placed your fate and future in the hands of this human. She knows you are the father of lies and that the truth is not in you. If you cannot convince her that you will completely comply with all of my commandments and never defy me again, then she has the duty to destroy you. You have one hour of their time to convince her."*

Before Christi could pray and ask God anything, He spoke to her in her mind. *"Oh Christi, you are my child whom I love. Know that I created you for this moment. Your heart is as pure as Satan's is evil. Your soul will know without a doubt if Satan can obey me as true God or if he is lying. I cannot end his existence without being untrue to my own word, which I cannot and will not do. That is why you are here at this moment and one reason for your creation. Satan has done everything he could do to destroy my creation of mankind and now his life is in your hands. The irony of the situation is not lost on him. But, I, God, have given you the power of life or death over him. If he cannot convince you, a mortal being, beyond a shadow of a doubt that he can be true and obey me without fail, then I command you to strike him down with your sword."*

Christi's mind spun with uncertainty. How could she make this decision by herself? She was being told by the God of the universe to judge one of the main forces of the

Bible and all prophesy. She was completely isolated from all of her elders and teachers who might have greater experience or knowledge in a matter like this. Her main source of correct action was God, but He had just told her to make this decision for Him.

She realized that she needed to put her understanding of things in order. God does not lie, ever.   God is always right. God had placed her in this position on purpose to meet requirements she could not even imagine. God told her that she would know without a doubt in her soul if Satan was lying now or even if he would change his mind in the future or if he would actually obey God's commandments for the rest of his time on Earth.

Therefore, based on her complete faith in God she would judge Satan and let him live to go to the Lake of Fire in a thousand years or terminate him now. WOW!

She turned her attention to the ultimate evil in the world and steeled herself. She said, "Satan, what do you have to say for yourself?"

Satan looked at Christi and said, "Don't speak to me you insignificant worm! I was the most powerful Angel in Heaven and I rule this world as I wish. I am privy to all the secrets of the universe and have knowledge beyond anything your puny mind can even conceive of. I speak only to God Himself!"

Christi nodded her head. "All you say is true except of our present relationship. Regardless of your over-inflated, egotistical view of things, the God who you bow your knee to has bound you and He has given me the authority, in

His name, to end your miserable existence if you cannot convince me that you will absolutely obey all His commandments for the rest of your days."

Christi jerked her glowing sword out of the ground and hefted it so that the point was directly aimed at Satan's throat. "Every word out of your mouth so far is convincing me that you will not humble yourself before your God and I can end this right now."

# CHAPTER TWENTY-SIX

The truth of the situation as stated by the human startled the devil like a wave of icy water being pored over his head. He wanted to roar his defiance and crush the life out of her but he could not move. He could see the esteem of Yahveh flowing off of the blade of her sword and knew that she had the capability of ending his existence at any second. And, although the situation was intolerable, it was real.

He carefully sensed her spirit and recoiled. He recognized the Son of God and God's Holy Spirit as integral components of this woman's spiritual makeup. She not only had the ability, she had the unquenchable fire and heart to do God's will. Normally, he would avoid her as a danger to himself. This time he wasn't able to do that. So he thought he might persuade her as he did the woman in the garden that God didn't really want her to kill him. He looked into her eyes and knew that women had come a long way since the garden. This woman would not be swayed by a simple misdirection because she didn't trust him or any word he might say.

Anger began to build in his heart against God for putting him in this situation. This wasn't his fault! He would use God's ways to derail this human's basis for true justice. A logical argument would put enough doubt in her mind that she would not kill him. Then he would deal with both her and God as he willed!

He made a simple argument in a smooth as syrup voice. "You do realize that your God is using you against me because He is incapable of killing me Himself? Why do you suppose that is? Have you ever wondered why I have existed these thousands of your years opposed to Him and He hasn't removed me by His own hand? Isn't it odd that he is so powerful yet incapable of doing this one thing?"

Christi listened to the devil's pitch with a knowledge base that Yahshua had enhanced for all the leaders of the Crossfire Team. She wasn't silly enough to go one-on-one with Satan and did not plan to get sucked into his logical snares. "I don't wonder about those things Lucifer. Because of God's loving nature He gave you safeguards even after you rebelled against Him in Heaven because he wanted you to be who you are in His plan. One of those safeguards was a promise to you that He would not destroy you by His own hand throughout the time He allotted to you on Earth. But that promise came with an agreement from you not to disobey His commandments."

"You trade on your reputation that you are the Father of Lies and therefore you think you are immune to any need to obey or use any restraint or even acknowledge God. Yes, it took thousands of years but you finally managed to offend God by your disobedience enough times that He has disowned you. I am honored to assist my God so that He doesn't have to break His word concerning the fate you have chosen for yourself. Your actions of continual disobedience no matter how many chances He has given you have put you in this situation. Yes, you may have been the highest Angel in heaven and you are thousands of years old. But, you act like a spoiled little brat of a child that doesn't understand, let alone give true love or respect. And now you only have thirty minutes left to convince me that you can truly change and obey God."

Satan realized this human had knowledge beyond the normal human being. He thought to himself, "More meddling by Yahshua no doubt. He has taken away more of my ability to turn this creature to my will. How unfair to me is this Son of God."

Satan stared daggers at the woman without effect. "I see that you have been well trained for this assignment. I am truly unable to come up with any argument or form of enticement that would sway you from killing me. I could actually tell you that I would obey God but you are not prepared to believe me or trust anything I say or offer. How am I supposed to convince you?"

Christi stared at the devil. "There must be something that would convince me or God would have simply told me to kill you when you showed up. I know, in your way of doing things it would be normal to extend suffering. But, God doesn't do that type of thing. He must believe that you could convince me somehow."

Satan thought furiously but nothing came to mind. "I normally don't tell the truth but in this case I'll make an exception. I truly cannot come up with a way to mount a convincing argument. It is humorous but, other than God I am the only entity that can't say, "The devil made me do it."

Christi thought about what the devil had said. "Maybe you have after all. You are not human, born to life. God made you and the other Angels to His standards. You are not creative and you can't beget offspring normally. But you could have introduced some bad code into your version of your own DNA. I'm only speculating here, but if you would humble yourself and honestly pray to God to fix only that part of your coding that causes you to; or does not prevent you from, violating God's commandments, you could continue on your evil path for a while longer. Why don't you give it a try? This truly is your last chance as you are almost out of time."

Satan considered the concept. He had to admit that way back in the farthest corners of his mind he too had questioned his escalating disobedience for a long time. He really, really did not want to seek help from God but like the human said, he was out of options. So he prayed that God would fix that part of his makeup so that he would cease his blatant disobedience. He realized that in a very small, tiny part of his heart he was sorry for doing that. As he waited for his fate he saw Christi smile. Then she faded out of his sight and his bonds fell away from him.

Satan shook his head. He guessed that God used that whole event to teach him some humility. He didn't know if God had "fixed" his DNA or not. As he prepared to go to his place within his domain; he heard one small word. "Remember". The thing that caught his mind was that the voice was that of the woman Christi, who was to have killed him. Not God, or Yahshua, but a human being was cautioning him.

He got back to thinking up something evil to do to her. "Then again, maybe I will wait a while before acting against her. Yes, that would be the more prudent path." Maybe God did do something to "fix" me. Hmmmm.

# CHAPTER TWENTY-SEVEN

Christi found herself back at her room on the "Sword". She knelt and prayed her thanks and love to God and to Yahshua for the entire event and especially the outcome. She took off her body armor and got undressed. She took a long hot shower to get every kind of demon stink off of her body. She had asked to see Raquel to make sure she was "spiritually" clean. She dried off and got dressed and was about to go to the armory when Raquel appeared in her room.

The mighty Archangel stepped up and put his hands on either side of her face. He stared into her eyes and then smiled as he stepped back. "You are spiritually clean Christi. Satan couldn't curse you or attach anything while he was bound. I salute you for everything you did."

Christi smiled, "Thank you Raquel. I wondered how you would feel after I helped Satan survive. I figured you probably hate him and would rejoice if I had killed him."

Raquel shook his head, "Christi, Angels don't *hate* anything or anybody. We're not wired like that. We are opponents and will fight to the death to beat them, but, we don't hate them. Actually I don't know what hate feels like. Anyway, like Jack says, "Hate is a destructive emotion for the person doing the hating as much or more than the one hated."

Christi looked at the Archangel, "Raquel, I was in the shower when I thought of asking Jack to call you to check on my spiritual health. How did you know to come this quickly?"

Raquel smiled, "Christi, you actually were praying for me to attend to you rather than just "thinking" about it."

Christi reddened slightly, "Well. I'm glad you waited until I was dressed, that would have been pretty embarrassing in the shower."

Raquel laughed, "Not really, we're not wired that way either. I waited because we are aware that if they are undressed it will upset humans when we appear. You are all right, Christi. The devil could not curse you while he was bound." He faded out of sight.

Christi laughed and grabbed her uniform and body armor and headed for the armory.

After cleaning it up and sending the other parts to the laundry she sat down at a table and started filling out her after-action report. She completed all of it including her trip to the demonic realm and her assignment from God and the results. Finishing up she looked around and then got up and asked the NCO manning the armory if any of the other team members had returned as yet.

Getting a negative response, she jogged to the War Room and found it empty also. She sat down and called Jack on the combat communications net.

Jack answered immediately. "Christi, I see you are in the War Room on the "Sword. Are you all right?"

Christi answered in the affirmative. "I was translated straight from the demonic realm to my apartment here on the ship. Is everything all right there at the university?"

Jack hesitated before answering. "We're not even in Israel anymore. With the exception of you, the entire team is headed for an island in the southern Atlantic Ocean. It seems one of the Albatross's divisions has teamed up with a large group of demons and is holding the island hostage."

Christi thought for a few seconds. "How about I suit up and get our Air Force to transport me to you in a Fragment?"

Jack chuckled, "How about you stay there and represent us on the ship until we get back? Contact the XO and the Captain to get filled in. Call me back when, or if, you need my help. Okay?"

Christi agreed and headed for the bridge of the "Sword" to find out what God had gotten her into now.

Receiving permission to enter the bridge she walked over to the XO's position and greeted Hugh Kelly. "Hi Commander Kelly, I'm Christi Steele and I'm a member of the Crossfire Core Team. Jack Malone asked me to check in with you and see what service the team can provide you."

The XO was a good judge of character and what he saw with Christi was a very intelligent and strong person that had confidence, assurance, and resilience in a solid package. A person who did not take themselves too highly and held others to the same standards she strived to meet. The fact that she was also a pretty woman who would not intentionally use her attractiveness as an asset to manipulate men and nor a license for familiarity from men or women. He liked her instinctively and smiled at her. "Hello Christi Steele, welcome to the bridge of the Sword."

Christi had reviewed Hugh Kelly's file and was intrigued to find the person lived up to his impressive background. "Thank you Commander, how can we be of service?"

Kelly pointed to a small table with two chairs next to it. They walked over and sat down. The commander grabbed a couple of cups and went to a coffee urn. He came back with two cups of coffee and some sugar and creamers. He gave Christi a cup and sat down with his hands around his cup. As Christi added some sugar she had a mini vision of Hugh Kelly sitting this way through endless nights at sea.

Hugh looked up at the young woman and smiled grimly. "We have a military-geopolitical problem that's above my pay grade and probably above Captain Conner's also. We have acquired a "shadow" that presents a myriad of issues for this ship. First off, it's a nuclear hunter-killer submarine. Second, it's a NWO-controlled ship. The New World Order is controlled by the Anti-Christ Marco Marino who doesn't like us and wants us eliminated. We cannot be destroyed by this shadow ship but we don't want to destroy it either. It is a new "Stryker" class American ship with several hundred American sailors and officers on it. It also has bubble cavitation capability which means it could be as fast as we are when we are submerged. We also don't want to expose our capabilities so that they can catalog us."

"We want to disengage without a battle but anything we do could be labeled as aggression which would call for a military response, escalation, and finally their destruction. They found us while we were on the surface and have continued to trail us for three days. The problem became acerbated this morning when we detected a second shadow. This one is an older Los Angeles class nuclear sub. We think they are preparing to call us out and demand the right to board us. We will not allow that, especially by a known hostile force. Again this will lead to demand escalation and finally combat." He smiled at Christi, since your team owns this ship, Captain Conners feels you need to make the hard decisions."

Christi prayed silently for several minutes. When Hugh grew restless she held up her hand requesting his patience. When she looked up she was nodding her head in agreement with the plan forming in her mind. "Show me our location and heading please."

Hugh stood up and Christi followed him over to the large plot board on the bridge. He pointed out their position and heading. They were sailing NNE toward the northern islands of Japan. Christi nodded, "Please show me all North Korean and Chinese naval forces and bases within one hundred nautical miles of our position."

Hugh passed the request to the rating manning the plot board. All sorts of new indications appeared on the board. Chinese ships and naval bases were shown in yellow and North Korean ships and facilities were in red.

Christi looked for the name she had been given. She found it and determined the distance. She asked Hugh "How long will it take us to reach this point here?"

Hugh shook his head. "We can get there in two hours but we don't want to do that. That is a supposedly "secret" Chinese Naval Base that is defended by the Chinese naval and air forces with great zeal. They will attempt to destroy... Ohh, I see what you are suggesting! We can disappear when they come thundering out of their base. Leaving only two American submarines where they shouldn't be."

Christi smiled, "That's only half of the plan Hugh. First off, I don't expect the American subs to actually follow us into the Chinese controlled waters. They are not that stupid. Secondly, we are going to not only become invisible but also go submerged and running flat out we will enter and leave those Chinese waters in less time than it takes for them to respond to the intrusion. That puts us into North Korean waters. We make a wide circle back out of those waters and head SSE through the Atlantic Ocean."

Hugh was grinning. "Not only will we lose our shadows and any possible aggression but we will create a whole new level of neuroses with the Chinese and the North Korean navies. Each one will think the other one has some new technology and it'll start a whole new arms race in the Far East."

Christi shook Hugh's hand, "I've got to make some calls and see if we can't make the Sword become a ghost the navies of the world simply can't locate or track."

The Commander nodded his head, "Somehow I think you will do just that. Christi, I am impressed. The solution you came up with would astound Naval Tacticians around the globe in its simplicity and multiple solutions. I had no idea you were that knowledgeable of naval warfare."

Christi smiled; "I'm simply a servant of the Most High God of the universe. He is the mastermind Hugh. Don't ever forget that and always give Him all the credit."

She transited back to the team quarters and went back to the War Room. Calling Jack, she told him everything was resolved. He thanked her and said they were heading back in the morning. Their assignment had also been resolved, permanently.

# CHAPTER TWENTY-EIGHT

Computing the twelve-hour time differences, Christi prayed for complete privacy on her communications. She then placed a call to Doctor Clashire in Denver Colorado in the United States of America. After explaining the events of the afternoon she asked if he had a solution to their visibility problem.

The Doctor asked if the line was secure. Christi said she wasn't sure but she felt it was being protected by God. Doctor Clashire sighed. "Christi, tell Jack I believe the OWG is about to confiscate his business here and arrest me. I won't take the mark of the beast and I expect to be terminated fairly quickly after I am apprehended."

Christi asked the Doctor to give her a few minutes. She prayed seriously for two minutes and got an answer. Doctor, I'm speaking for Jack. Do you still have one of the Force Generators?"

Byron smiled to himself, "For some unknown reason I kept a single old unit just in case. Are you concerned about it being captured?

" Christi said, "No, I want you to get the Force Generator, put it on, and activate it immediately." Byron did as she asked and felt the tingly sensation. Christi smiled, "The forces you're talking about are on their way to the plant right now. With that unit on you will be safe until I can get there."

"Okay," the doctor replied. "Also, I have completely destroyed all documentation concerning these units including research and computer information. Everything else was shipped out weeks ago. I can promise you that the computer systems have been thoroughly scrubbed."

Christi sighed, "Bryon, how about your family?"

"My wife passed away last year and I have no other living relatives. We never had children and I am a fairly private person."

Christi said, "All right, I will be there in two hours to pick you up at the plant. Go out front at exactly noon your time. See you then." She broke the connection and called

Rob at the Crossfire Team Air Force quarters. "Rob, this is Christi Steele. The rest of the team will not be back until tomorrow morning and we have an emergency." She explained about Doctor Clashire and asked to use a Fragment to rescue him. Rob told her to come down to the hanger area.

Once there, she met Rob and he told her both of the Fragments were out with the other team members but he would personally take her to Colorado. He led her to the "Formidable". The plane was huge!

Rob contacted the bridge and had the Sword slow down, rise to the surface while still moving at a good speed. He was able to be lifted onto the deck and launch the Formidable very quickly. As they rose out of the area Rob could see the Sword had disappeared again and there were North Korean jets headed their way. He lifted the nose of the warbird and headed for space. The vertical rise speed of the Formidable quickly became so great the Korean jets broke off the chase adding to their confusion.

Rob regaled Christi with tales of previous combats until they approached Jack's plant on the south side of Denver. As the clock reached noon Rob lowered the Formidable to the ground in front of the plant buildings. As they dropped, Rob could see there were many troops surrounding Byron Clashire. They were trying, completely unsuccessfully; to keep him from moving toward the plane. Christi exited the plane, ignored the troops, and walked over to the doctor. She greeted him and then walked him over to the aircraft and started to cycle him through the Field Generator field surrounding the plane. An Abrams tank fired a shell at the plane. Its energy was absorbed by the fields surrounding Christi, Doctor Clashire, and the plane. The round exploded, doing, absolutely nothing.

All at once, a huge demon appeared and ran up to the plane. It slashed at Christi with its large black sword. Christi had automatically started praying and her golden armor and her sword appeared. She used her left hand to shove Byron Clashire completely into the plane which made him doubly protected. She turned and blocked a second blow by the demon's sword. Raising her blade vertically, and being on the plane's stairs, she rose up and struck downward. The brilliant blade of Christi's sword shattered the dull black blade of the demon as it put the blade above its head and her blade continued downward through the demon's head and body until it stopped in the middle of the demon's chest.

As it began to dissolve, four more demons appeared out of the rift and moved toward the plane to attack Christi.

Rob used four chain guns on the Formidable to rake the new demons. Unfortunately, these four were legally present and ignored the attack. Several soldiers fired on the demons and two demons changed direction so that they could attack the soldiers. The troops had no defense and the demons quickly hacked several of them to death,

As the slaughter continued, Christi dispatched the demon fighting her and ran to the defense of the soldiers. She had just destroyed those two when a dozen more demons came out of the rift and attacked her. She prayed that God would help her defeat the new ones.

Raquel and Caleb appeared and took the battle to the demons. Fighting in unison with Christi, the two Angels helped eliminate the remaining demons. Christi was just breathing a sigh of relief when a large demon came out of the rift. This one was far more powerful than the others.

It used its sword to knock a tank out of its way. Turning on the Angels it also battered Raquel and Caleb, knocking them to one side as it engaged Christi.

Christi couldn't strike this demon because its blade didn't shatter and it was so strong it kept her blade away from its body. It smashed at Christi four times but could not overcome the Force Generator field.

Raquel backed up and spoke, "Nasgulor, you have no authority to enter the human dimension. Return to your place in the second heaven, Now!"

The powerful demon laughed, "Raquel, I don't speak to low-life beings such as you. Be gone or I will destroy you along with this pathetic female."

About that time Rob lifted the Formidable off the ground and rotated it to line up with the demonic rift. The Atomic Canon fired four times directly into the rift. The glare of the nuclear explosions lit up the world inside the rift and power of the explosions forced the rift to collapse and the opening snapped shut.

Nasgulor screamed in anger and attacked the plane. He couldn't damage it so he turned on Christi and raised his sword again.

Christi heard the quiet voice of Yahshua as the Son of God spoke to Nasgulor, *"Nasgulor! Why have you violated God's commandments and deliberately entered this dimension?"*

The giant demon angrily responded, "It is you who have violated our covenant and given the human scum these shields and swords. God has no right to do that! I will not tolerate this. . ."

There was a blinding flash of light and a heavy rumble of a thundering noise and Nasgulor disappeared. The Lord said, *"God will do whatever He sees as right and necessary. You have blasphemed against God by deciding in your mind what He can or cannot do. Not even Satan dares to do that. Therefore, you are condemned to the abyss until you are judged at the end of time. Your future is the Lake of Fire.*

Christi raised her sword as a salute to the two Angels and to the troops that had fought for her. She knelt and praised God and Yahshua for the victory. Climbing to her feet she walked over and entered the plane that had landed.

Rob lifted the Formidable off the ground in the profound silence that the voice of Yahshua had generated in all the troops. Rob opened up the engines and they left the area of the city in less than two minutes, the state in five minutes and the United States in twelve minutes.

# CHAPTER TWENTY-NINE

After the Formidable had been recovered by the Sword, Christi reported to the newly returned Jack and Mark and let them introduce Doctor Clashire to the rest of the team and the crew of the Sword while she repeated her earlier routine of getting cleaned up, taking her stuff to the armory, and generating her after action reports.

She wanted to get some sleep but knew she needed to explain her actions of the last thirty-three hours to the team leaders. She walked into the War Room and received a standing ovation from the entire Core Team.

After she thanked everyone and sat down at her position, Jack spoke up. "Christi, after reviewing the videos from your body armor and reading your reports I have to congratulate you on your victories in every area. You exemplified courage, bravery, and exceptional wisdom in your meeting with Satan. Immediately after being translated by God back to the Sword you were able to act on our behalf and resolve the knotty problems of the American submarines shadowing our ship. By the way, I received a glowing report from Captain Conners and Commander Kelly that rates you very highly."

Jack cleared his throat. "Then, you single handedly devised a solution that provided a safe rescue of Byron Clashire from the One World Government troops and a flood of demons in Colorado."

"Everything you did was correct and shows a level of leadership unparalleled in my knowledge by anyone who hasn't even finished their training and has had only a limited amount of experience to date. I believe I know the answer but would you explain why you didn't feel it was necessary to discuss any of these actions with us before you acted?"

Christi was still warm from all the accolades for her efforts and didn't feel concerned by Jack's question. "The answer is simple. Initially, I was commanded to find and confront Satan by God. I wasn't given an opportunity to reach out to the leadership for direction or advice. While I was confronting Satan I was commanded by God to judge the devil by his own words. I desperately wanted any or all of you guys to tell me what to do. Again, there was no opportunity to ask."

Christi smiled, "After I returned and contacted you, your direction was to seek out the Captain and the XO and offer the team's services. When I was presented with the immediate problem of the escalating confrontation with the American submarines I prayed and God told me exactly what to say and do. Again, I had no chance to contact you. Lastly, when I contacted Doctor Clashire to seek his help in preventing more confrontations with the world's sea powers I was faced with the time-critical situation of probably losing him and his life if I didn't act right then and there. In short, in each case I knew if I was able to reach you on how to respond to each of these situations your answer would have been to pray and find out what God wanted us to do. So I did that again."

"I prayed and did what the Father told me to do. Each time I prayed I did check with Him to see if I should seek your advice before doing everything I did. God told me to do what He said and He, God, would include you in His plans directing my actions."

"I apologize for not involving you in these Team efforts as this is your team, and yours not mine, to make such decisions and I affected the whole team by my actions. Therefore, I ask you all to forgive me and know that I will always seek your inputs in the future."

Jack smiled, "What you did and your motives for doing them the way you did does not require forgiveness from me or any of us on the team. You acted in the highest order to walk in the fear and admonition of the Lord our God. I can honestly say that I could not have done any better than what you did because that is the truth."

"Every person of the Crossfire Team acts as children and servants of Yahshua and Yahveh God. You were correct in that I did hear from God during this time that you were humble and obedient throughout this period of training. When I was praying for you and asking if one of us should have been there for you, God reminded me that it was His decision to translate you back to the ship so that He could rely on you, not us, in these events. That was humbling for me and made me realize that God does what He will with you and everyone else and that I needed to understand I am not as necessary to the team operations as I think I am. It is His team after all."

Mark stood up at his position and pointed at Christi, "I declare your training complete and want to talk to you about your time with old sparky."

That resulted in a lot of laughter and calls for a party to celebrate Christi's graduation.

# CHAPTER THIRTY

Mark and Sarah were in the process of searching for any more activities of the Albatross or demons when Jack interrupted them. "Guys, I think we need to sit down with Carol, Hugo, and either Rose or Caleb concerning our next target after the Albatross."

Mark nodded his head, "Agreed, we're coming up empty here."

Jack called Carol to meet them in the large Conference room/Dining room as he prayed for spiritual assistance from the Angels.

Carol walked in and greeted Jack and the Connellys and took a seat. Laura dropped in to ask a question of Mark on the training schedule when the Heavenly contingent showed up. Jack was surprised to see Raquel and three other powerful Archangels rather than Hugo and their normal Angels.

The new Archangels stood there staring at the five humans as they evaluated the team members using senses, powers, and information that were way beyond human understanding.

Mark tolerated that scrutiny for several minutes in silence and then asked, "Can we be of any service to you and your co-workers Raquel?"

The most powerful-looking of the new Archangels looked at Raquel. "This one is as aggressive as you indicated. I think I like him. I see why Satan has fits about him."

Mark smiled, "Just in case your Spidey sense isn't working at full blast, this "one's" name is "Mark"."

Raquel knew both the Angel and Mark well enough to step in at this point before things got completely out of control. He seemed to grow in stature and authority and stepped between the two groups. His voice was louder, clearer, and stronger. "Allow me to introduce everyone!"

The strongest new Archangel smiled at Raquel. "The time has not come for that, Raquel, not yet." He turned to Mark and the other team members. "We appreciate this opportunity to meet with you all. I apologize if my manner is unsettling to you." His eyes seemed to burn right through Mark. I am somewhat unused to dealing with the human dimension. We will meet again, soon, in combat against our mutual enemy and until then I will seek to improve my communication skills. Things will also go better if you would consider improving your manners."

The three Archangels disappeared.

Mark shook his head, "How come I can get along with you and the other Angels, but this guy talks over me as if I am the one with issues while I'm right here?"

Raquel sighed, "I am the one that needs to apologize to all of you. I should have given you advance notice of my guests and their, somewhat, odd way of doing and expressing themselves. Actually, I didn't do either because they showed up just as I was headed your way."

The Archangel sighed again. "Let me explain. The spokesman for that Heavenly trio is named "Raziel". He is a fierce warrior for heaven. He has personally accounted for over one hundred and thirty thousand demon terminations in his six thousand years. Most of his time on Earth has been in battle with Satan's demons and Archdemons. In those early days, humans weren't educated and feared Angels and demons alike, for the last several centuries he has been accustomed to not speaking to or actually having any interaction with humans. He is greatly feared by demons and also by many people, especially the unsaved mass of humanity. His name since the very first humans appeared on Earth means "Secret of God" and he is privy to all of the secrets of the God of the universe."

"The second Archangel was the "Michael" of the Bible. He is also the protecting Angel of Law Enforcement and the military."

"I'm not at liberty to discuss the third Archangel at this time. I can tell you that "Raziel" was impressed by you, Mark. That is the first time I've ever heard him apologize to anyone but the Most High. Mark, I cannot stress enough that you amend your attitude while talking to Raziel. He can be a great friend but an even greater opponent. And, I would have to referee any contention between you two and I am not looking forward to that."

Mark was serious, "I too, must apologize to you for my attitude and I will ask Raziel for his forgiveness for my lack of manners when I see him next. I also assure you I am, and will be much more respectful of him next time we meet." Raquel nodded.

Laura asked, "What does your name mean Raquel?"

Raquel smiled slightly, my name is also spelled "Raguel" and it means "Friend of God. My duties include being the overseer for all the other Archangels and Angels in Heaven or on Earth."

Sarah whistled, "Wow! You are so humble I never guessed you were so highly placed in heaven. Thank you for all your efforts concerning our small part of God's plan."

Raquel laughed, "I am honored to call all of you my friends and thank you for your appreciation of my little efforts to assist you."

Raquel faded away before Jack could ask him about the near future for the team.

Sarah patted Mark on his arm and said, "Thank you for taking the high road in your disagreement with Raziel."

Mark shrugged, "Well, I really kind of had to because I had no idea of who he was let alone the fact that he was not just being rude and superior but is simply socially ignorant."

Sarah sighed and made a wry face, "Mark, I really don't think that would be your best argument to get along with an Archangel who is much older and wiser, not to mention much stronger than you and whose attack would not cause your armor and sword to appear."

Mark grinned, "There is that, but better yet is the fact that both of us dislike Satan more than anything else. His enemy is my enemy and I will work with him regardless of our social capabilities."

# CHAPTER THIRTY-ONE

Mark, Jack, Laura, and Sarah talked about all the permutations and possibilities but essentially came up with nothing new. Jack led them in a prayer for enlightenment and guidance. No voices, Angels, or words. They split up to manage their workloads of training, design, and team and crew issues.

Around ten thirty in the evening Mark was headed back to summarize his training sessions at the War Room when he stepped onto soft grass and saw a fantastic vista spread out before him. He had been translated to Heaven enough times he wasn't surprised by the sudden change in surroundings. He stopped and looked around and was pleased by the sights he saw.

An angelic figure was approaching him from a distance but was traveling quickly and neared his position in a few seconds. Raziel was looking grim and had his right hand on his sword hilt as he stared at Mark.

Mark stared back at the Archangel and simply waited to see what would develop. Raziel nodded his head, "Good, I sense no fear in you."

Mark smiled faintly, "Raziel, I've stood toe-to-toe with Satan two times when all he wanted was my death. Yahveh is my strength and my joy. I'm not afraid of death or any enemy. I respect them and their abilities because they are dangerous, but as a fellow warrior I expect no evil from God's warriors and messengers. You summoned me so how can I help you?"

Raziel laughed, "Well-spoken Mark Connelly. In truth, your team summoned me by your prayers for guidance. I responded to that prayer rather than Raguel because the trail your team has blazed through the Anti-Christ's chosen armies has caused him to look for assistance from Satan to employ an old enemy of which I have far more experience than the other angels."

Mark smiled and sat down on the grassy area. "I appreciate you using your valuable time to work with us. And, as I told Raquel, I want to apologize for my bad manners during our first encounter. That was rude and disrespectful of me and I ask for your forgiveness."

The eons old Archangel nodded, "I accept your apology and I, of course, forgive you. Now, let's talk about an extremely old demonic force which is about to be resurrected and released into the human dimension by Satan. Marco Marino requested this force specifically to destroy your team and the other eleven teams like yours operating on the Earth at this time."

Mark thought about the implications of an ages-old demonic spirit force recreated and released on the Earth by the resident evil on the Earth. "What was the origin of this threat? How do we combat it?"

Raziel nodded his head as he recognized a kindred spirit. Mark was direct and to the point of how to destroy the threat. No phony chest beating or proclamations of superiority just a request for strategic information. "The origin of this being was on Earth before mankind was created. A race called the Nephilim ruled the planet. The Nephilim were a race of fallen angels prior to the time of Satan's revolt. They were exceptionally large, violent, and long-lived. They rejected their creator God and God thereby cursed them. They were evil incarnate and God finally destroyed the last of their kind in the great flood when Noah was allowed to use the Ark to continue life on Earth."

"The problem is that the Nephilim had spirits like humans and spirits are eternal. The being Satan plans to revive and embody is named "Xndalius" and was a fierce fighter in his day. I am privy to all the secrets of God and I still don't understand how Satan is going to attempt to restore Xndalius but I do know how he can bring him into this present time."

Mark was worried by the anxiety shown by Raziel concerning this creature. If an experienced Archangel was shook up by this creature it boded badly for the Crossfire Team. "What was this creature capable of in its previous life in battle?"

Raziel frowned, "Mostly invincible, nigh well indestructible and unstoppable. I fought against it once when I was in my prime. I had beaten three Archdemons in one battle and routed over three hundred demons in a single day. I came up against Xndalius and in a single blow he disabled me and smashed me to the ground. Then, instead of killing me, he laughed at me and moved on with the battle. It was very humiliating and defeating in my line of work."

Mark could sense the pain that action caused the archangel in his voice. "That must have been a low point in your life. I've been embarrassed and humiliated in my service career and it is defeating. Other than sheer size and strength what makes this creature so invincible?"

Raziel sighed, "It seems to have some form of natural ability to counteract the power of God. Honestly, I don't understand how anything could stand against God in this universe. I can assure you that the sword, shield, and armor that your team is anointed with would not be effective against Xndalius as he was before. This indestructible shield that God has given you may be the one thing that can keep the creature from damaging you but it doesn't seem to be an offensive weapon that could defeat it."

Mark shrugged his shoulders. " We will have to see how effective it is against Xndalius in his new form. What has God said about this counteraction capability?"

Raziel shook his head, "Nothing at all. I inquired about it several times before the flood with no response."

# CHAPTER THIRTY-TWO

Mark returned to the Sword after assuring Raziel that they would work on finding a way to stop Xndalius if Satan was able to resurrect the creature and launch it on the world. He walked into the War Room and brought Jack, Laura, and David up to speed on the next possible challenge to their existence.

Jack agreed with Mark that it was very odd that God wouldn't communicate with Raziel about this capability of Xndalius to neutralize God's weapons. Jack decided that he would pray, fast, and deeply seek God about this problem. Either that or the entire team could be going to Heaven earlier than the midpoint of the seven-year Tribulation period.

There were several incursions by demons over the next week that required team involvement but nothing outside of the ordinary. The entire team had a chance to stand down and rest for the first time in many months.

Training goals were met and everything on the ship was cleaned at least twice. Competitive sports such as racquetball and volleyball games kept everyone toned up. Laura liked the fact that there were no on-lookers; everyone took turns playing and rooting each other on. Rabbi Epstein was busy integrating the Jewish Feasts and community life into everyone's schedules.

Jack stayed with the team schedules while following a Daniel Fast and seeking the Lord in prayer frequently throughout the twenty-four-hour cycle on board their mobile base. He hadn't received anything about the new enemy as yet but wasn't discouraged. He knew it would be handled in God's time.

On the twentieth day of praying and fasting; Jack knelt in prayer in the bedroom of their suite and was praying his love to the Lord when he was transported to Heaven in the spirit.

While everywhere he had been in Heaven up until now had been tranquil and soothing to the soul and spirit this place was filled with the aura of God's judgment and very military in tone. Actually, if the last four years of Jack's life hadn't been filled with combat this surrounding could be frightening and ominous.

The Angel Hugo who had trained the team members in many things was standing a short distance away so Jack walked over to him. "Greetings Hugo, I'm glad to see you again, it's been too long between your visits."

Hugo smiled as he thought "Real praise and friendship from his human students was a rare thing, something to be treasured." "Hello Jack Malone, I bring you knowledge from the Most High. Now hear the Word of the Lord. *"Jack, I've heard your petition to understand the ability of Xndalius to overcome the weapons I've given your team to do battle with the forces of darkness. You have humbled yourself to hear from me so I will tell you what you want to know. Recall Hugo's training about the power of righteousness and unrighteousness and how a more powerful unrighteousness can overcome an Angel's or a human's righteousness and defeat them? Good, that is the power of Xndalius. This being was so evil and violently against My authority that his level of unrighteousness exceeded Raziel's righteousness and allowed him to defeat my Archangel. If they met today the outcome would be the same. I intervened and kept Raziel from destruction at that time. It wasn't Raziel the Archdemon was laughing at but he was laughing at me because I had to step in to save Raziel. You will have an advantage over a resurrected Xndalius because the Force Generator field is a part of me and carries my righteousness which the demon cannot overcome. Talk to Doctor Clashire about weaponizing the field to allow you to do combat with Xndalius. It was available, and still is available but needs to be released and understood. Remind him of how his first models could affect things at a distance before he modified it. Go in my name and I will be with you."*

Jack thanked Hugo and watched everything vanish and be replaced by his bedroom.

Jack prayed his gratitude to Yahveh in Yahshua's name and then got up and headed to the War Room. On his way he called Mark and asked him to locate Doctor Clashire and bring him to the War Room.

# CHAPTER THIRTY-THREE

When Mark walked in with Doctor Byron Clashire Jack was at a conference table off to one side of the large meeting area and waved them over. After greetings and getting settled, Jack asked Byron if he could work on modifying the Force Generator with what he had available on the team's ship, the "Sword".

The doctor nodded his head, "Oh yes, I transferred all my research to the computers on the ship when I arrived. I cannot tell you how much more advanced these new computers are over what I had to work with at the company in Colorado. I also have a wonderful working relationship with your young Mr. Crayton who seems more than willing to do all the hard work which frees me up to work on the theoretical aspects. I really want to meet him and find out where he received his education. He has been able to keep up with me and that is something nobody else has been able to do in my lifetime."

Jack and Mark traded smiles. Mark put his hand on Byron's shoulder. "Byron, I think Ethan Reaper is pulling your leg somewhat. Our resident Computer and Security Center Manager has a sense of humor that sometimes overrides his common sense. Crayton isn't a person but is a complex assistance program developed by the previous manager, Charlie Wu, who considered the program as his alter ego. Sometimes it seems almost human in its responses."

The Doctor sat back in his chair and considered his new understanding. "Well then, I guess meeting a program in person is out of the question so I will enjoy working with Crayton by computer. I would like a chance to meet Mr. Wu when we can. Now, what are the modifications you need?"

Jack explained what God told him and then went over the comments with the Doctor. His words to me were: "Talk to Doctor Clashire about weaponizing the field to allow you to do combat with Xndalius. It was available, and still is available but needs to be released and understood.

Remind him of how his first models could affect things at a distance before he modified it."

Byron sat there and shook his head. "I know exactly what God is talking about. I believe the more I learn about what I thought I was "fixing" the more I realize I was trying to work in my knowledge rather than bow as I should have to the Great Designer, Sorry."

Jack laughed, "Bryon, it is all right, don't beat yourself up, your understanding of God is a journey not an event. We've all fallen in that area. How long will it take you to restore this capability?"

Byron looked up and smiled, "I believe I can restore that function by this afternoon. The problem is that I have no concept of what it does and how to control it. I'm also concerned about testing this "weapon" function inside of a submarine or even on a surfaced ship. Remember how damaging the simple "move" feature was?"

Jack nodded, "Good point Doctor. I will pray about these questions while you are working. Try to not "Activate" the function before we know what we're releasing."

Jack prayed that God would make all the information on how to use this new "feature" available to him so that they could do His work in defending His people. Again he found himself in the strange area of Heaven and meeting with the Angel Hugo.

"Greetings again Hugo, I hope I'm not pestering you too much about this situation."

Hugo's deep voice held a hint of humor in it. "You are doing God's will in this matter and we could not have a better reason to meet.

Hugo studied Jack as he began his explanation. "Concerning this Force Generator "weapon" your Doctor Clashire was absolutely correct about not using it on water craft, especially one that is submerged."

"The thing about this "weapon" is not only its unlimited range but its unlimited energy level. I saw an early version of this "activated" for only an instant. It annihilated several demons and the rock formations in front and behind them. But, it also destroyed the entire landscape for the next three miles because the user failed to define the target properly."

"I do believe a serious application of this force could bore through the planet and still destroy anything in its path on the other side. I find it even more concerning that the Most High would allow humans to wield this power without stringent limitations"

Jack sighed, "And yet, the Most High told me to bring this force to life and to use it against this "unstoppable" enemy."

Hugo nodded, "Well then, let's get started. You know the passages in the Bible in Genesis 1:3, 1:6, 1:9, and 1:14 where it states *"And God said, Let there be*?" When Jack nodded, Hugo continued. "That was how God created the world; He spoke it and the rest of the universe into existence. This weapon uses the same power to un-create whatever the user wants to destroy."

Hugo looked closely at Jack. "Do you understand that this "weapon" uses the same fundamental power that created the whole universe but in reverse!"

Jack suddenly felt weak and inadequate to use such a power. "I do understand, Hugo, but I am concerned about having such ultimate power in my control. What if I make a mistake or agents of Satan get control of it? It would be catastrophic!"

Hugo was nodding his head, "My feelings precisely." But, as you have stated, God has spoken and it is going to be in your hands soon. Please be very careful how you use it. When the power is available you absolutely have to focus it on the target. You will have the power words, *"In the name and by the authority of Yahveh God, I destroy this single creature!"* You absolutely must focus your thoughts on that creature before you speak the power words. Otherwise you could destroy all single creatures on Earth or possibly, in the entire universe!"

Hugo said, "I will pray for God's guidance for you. Be very aware that having control of this power could give you delusions of being like God Himself. Don't fall into that super ego trap or else Satan could have control of you and through you, the power." With that parting thought Hugo and Heaven disappeared.

Jack prayed that God would take this test away from him, because it could be more than he should have in his hands. He felt the Father's nearness and His confidence in him.

# CHAPTER THIRTY-FOUR

Jack used his comm link to contact Doctor Clashire. "Doctor, Modify only the Field Generator in my body armor. There absolutely cannot be any more FGs with this weapon modification, none. Do you understand me?"

The Doctor answered, "Loud and clear Jack. I have already made the change to your FG in your body armor. What should I do with your armor until you need it?"

"Give it to Mark and have him take it to the vault area and lock it in the special vault immediately!"

"Mark, do you copy?" Mark answered in the affirmative and immediately took Jack's body armor to the special vault and secured it.

Jack called a meeting with the Core Team in the War Room. When all fourteen members were present, he prayed for a Holy Spirit covering over the meeting that would prevent any form of demonic eavesdropping or viewing of the meeting or its contents. He looked at the assembled group of battle tested warriors that he trusted with his life. "What I am about to tell you must stay a complete secret within this group. The potential for catastrophe if the wrong forces know about this is absolute. As you know we, as a team, have been tasked by Yahveh God to stop the forces of the Anti-Christ working in union with Satan. Up until now we have accomplished that task aided by God's gifts of the armor and sword and on special occasions, the Force Generator field. As in all arms races each side in the war escalates the conflict by introducing a more powerful force or weapon to give them the advantage. Well, through witchcraft and necromancy Satan is bringing back to existence a creature from the time before man walked the Earth. This demon was so powerfully unrighteous that it could destroy Archangels in battle. Our armor and swords will be ineffectual against this force. While it is assumed that our Force Generators are of a sufficient level of God's power and righteousness that the creature cannot destroy us we don't know what enhancements or improvements Satan may give this creature along with a physical body.

Even if our FGs can keep us safe we still did not have any way to stop this creature and survive that battle, until today."

Jack knew this information was critical to these people and wanted to prepare them. "Our Father Yahveh has placed into my hands a power so terrible that I could easily destroy this entire planet. I tell you this not to brag on how important or powerful I am; but to ask every one of you to understand how terrifying it is to me to have control of this power. When we encounter this creature I am pleading with you all to pray to God in Yahshua's name to empower me to use this "weapon" to destroy this threat to our team and the others like us. And to then to immediately give this capability back to God. Basically, I am very aware that the more power a person has the more it can corrupt him to abuse the use of it. This is an ultimate power that could easily ultimately corrupt me. I know that God has confidence in my ability to resist that corruption, still I am scared by the temptation it presents and my possible weakness just because I have it."

Jack looked at the silent assembly. "I am open to suggestions, comments, or other considerations."

Nobody said a word for several minutes. Then Mark stood up, "Jack, I can honestly say that there is no one else that I would feel safer having access to such a power than you. I believe the Father doesn't make mistakes and He selected you for this burden before the world began. I will support you one hundred percent and I will be praying for your ability to do it right when push comes to shove." Mark then slowly started to clap his hands to applaud him. The rest of the Core Team got to their feet and joined Mark in thunderous applause. Jack felt the tears roll down his face and smiled at this show of support.

Jack felt warm hands on his back and found Laura and Sarah standing behind him and crying with him in support and happiness for him.

Mark adjourned the meeting as a formality even though no one left and were all busy discussing the revelation and coming battle.

Jack left and sought out Doctor Clashire. "Byron, tell me how I activate that weapon's power."

The Doctor looked at Jack with sympathy. "Before I tell you how, I want to thank you for saving me from falling into a great sin. I don't know exactly how powerful this weapon is or how it does whatever it does, but after I corrected the generator in your body armor I suddenly felt like it was put in my hands to correct several grievous and unholy problems in the world today. Such as an evil regime that is killing thousands of innocent people each year and is growing in power. To know that I could do what needs to be done to stop them was almost impossible to resist. You saved me by having Mark take it away and lock it out of my reach before I could decide to act. Just having that inability to use that power made me realize how insidious that power was. I love all of the team and especially you. But, if I had continued to be in the thrall of that power I was ready to eliminate you, Mark, and anyone else who came between me and possession of that power. The thought that I would even consider doing something like that frightened me so much I dropped to my knees and pleaded with God to prevent me from ever having anything to do with such power again. He comforted me and assured me that I would never have that problem again. He means what He says. I have no concept in my mind as to what I did to activate that power and can never do it again."

Jack sighed, "I'm sorry that you had to go through that Byron. Like you I'm just a human being and to have God-like power is probably beyond our ability to use it correctly. Still, I have to believe that Yahveh will always be in control and would have prevented you from misusing His power. I also have to believe He will only allow me to use it for this one express purpose."

Byron looked at Jack with a thought that encouraged him. "Was it really that much power?"

Jack nodded his head; This is the reverse of God's speaking the entire universe into being. You were wise to ask for it to be gone in your future. Anyway, did God leave you the method to bring it on line?"

Byron sighed and smiled, "Just push the new blue switch."

# CHAPTER THIRTY-FIVE

Carol kept a tight watch on the matrix for any hint of a new effort by Satan to attack the Crossfire Team. But, it wasn't her who sounded the first alert. A phone call from the team in Spain rang the warning bells on the Sword.

Jack took the call and listened to the Spanish team leader tell about running into a super demon that they couldn't stop. It killed four of their team despite their armor and swords. Apparently none of their team was able to touch it and when they prayed for angelic support none of the angels would do battle with this demon.

Jack and Laura were sure this was the first interaction with Xndalius. They also knew that there was little time until they battled Satan's super demon. Jack announced to all team members what happened to the Spanish Team and warned them to be on guard to avoid battle with this new demon.

Carol called a warning into the War Room because she saw the type of setup battle they had discussed in the Core Team meetings. "The enemy is asking for permission to bring thirty demons into Israel tomorrow at noon to attack the portal area to the undersea base. It looks like a deliberate effort to engage the Team. That is because the request is to allow for an attack on the Crossfire Team. The devil knows we aren't based there anymore but obviously expects us to defend that area of Tel Aviv."

At ten-thirty Jack took his body armor out of the vault and donned it. He looked with a little trepidation at the new blue switch next to the Field Generator switch at the right side of the collar. It certainly didn't look that important. But he took great care that he didn't accidently switch it to the "on" position.

They were in position with an IDF backup when a rift opened up and some double-ugly demons came boiling out looking for a fight. The total fight lasted forty minutes until all the demons were dispatched to the abyss and the rift closed.

On the flight back to their ship Jack and Mark decided it was a trial run to see if the Team would respond. If so, then another battle would be announced soon.

By the time they had cleaned up and completed their after action reports Carol announced that there was a new request for an identical attack the next day.

Jack looked at Mark, "There is something funny here; it's just too easy to figure out what they are doing."

The next day at noon a rift opened up at the same place and six demons, uglier than those the day before rushed out and only found seven team members waiting for them. A distant eighth member, Carol Moffet, weighed in with her sniper rifle laying head shot on every demon. Five of the six died before reaching the battle line and that one was dispatched by Mark quickly.

Then a large demon came out of the rift full of confidence and aloofness. Mark commented, "This looks like your special of the day, Jack".

Jack studied the newcomer and was about to use the blue switch when everything went black. Jack couldn't see anything. He used the comm net and told everyone to fall back toward the portal as they could. He heard Carol's 50 caliber sniper rifle so he knew she could see to shoot. He knew he couldn't use the blue switch because he could not target the creature. Everyone went as fast as possible back toward the portal with Jack. They gathered together and Mark looked at the blur that was Jack, "I didn't expect this. Think they know about your need to focus?"

Jack responded, "I really don't know, Mark. It is hampering us but I think it's not working too well for them either. Otherwise they would have attacked us by now if they could.

The IDF Commander called Mark to see if they were all close to the portal. When Mark told him that they were all there the Commander had his troops with the heavy machine guns' open fire on the rest of the darkness and enfilade the area. When the large demon was seen the IDF fired a tank cannon at it. The blast blew the demon back about thirty feet but otherwise didn't affect it.

The darkness ended just as suddenly as it started. But, the demons were gone and the rift wasn't there any longer. Mark called it a day and the team flew back to the ship.

For the next four days there were no more scheduled attacks. Jack continued to fast and pray for God's guidance. On Wednesday, five days after the last attack Jack heard from God. The Angel Rose brought him God's word. *"Jack, your prayers are a sweet music to me. I treasure every word. Now, I will tell you, so that later you will know that I am God. Soon, Xndalius will attack you and it is in your hand to destroy him. Do so! Do not fear, I will be with you."*

Jack thought to call Mark when Rose stopped him. Her face was sad and she held out her hand to him. "I also bring you a challenge from Satan which I wish I did not have to do."

Jack felt the depths of the black chasm stretching out below him as he had felt when Father God first called him and Laura into His service in a Men's Clothing Store in Denver, Colorado in the U.S. years and hundreds of battles ago. He no longer felt concerned or frightened as he had then. He smiled at the beautiful Angel. "Do not feel saddened by this task Rose. It is the Will of the Most High that you tell me what the enemy of all mankind and all Angels has conjured up this time. I look forward to this challenge as God has prepared me to meet it."

Rose was actually startled by Jack's confidence. "Satan wants Mark Connelly to meet him in individual combat against his chosen champion. The price for not meeting this challenge will be the death of all eight hundred men and women who are stranded on a cruise ship off of the Israeli coast. The combat will be on the cruise liner at noon tomorrow. No delays will be accepted. He wants an agreement immediately."

Jack prayed that God's Holy Spirit would give him the right words. He told Rose, "Tell Satan that Mark Connelly doesn't consider this challenge worthy of his time since he has already bested Satan himself several times. Tell Satan that I will meet his champion in combat tomorrow at noon on the cruise liner. If his champion can defeat me, then Mark will fight with him. Tell Satan that this condition is non-negotiable and if he doesn't accept it then we are not interested in playing his little games."

Rose was shocked by Jack's attitude and lack of concern over the lives of that many people. "Jack! You must know that Satan will kill all those people if Mark doesn't..."

Jack stared at Rose. "How many years have you dealt with this evil spirit? You, of all Angels should know that Satan is only on this world to steal, kill, and destroy! Those people will be killed if Mark shows up or not. Satan is a liar and the truth is not in him. Tell him what I have said. I will meet this "champion" of evil in the Name of Yahveh God tomorrow at noon."

Rose shook her head. "You don't understand, Jack! This champion is beyond my ability to fight, not even Raquel dares to meet him in combat. Why do you want to throw your life away?"

Jack was about to answer the Angel when God spoke gently to Rose. *"Jack is My Champion, Rose. Do as he ask and see My mighty right hand prevail."*

Rose bowed at the waist, "As you command, God." She looked oddly at Jack and whirled out of sight in a flash of gold and brilliant white.

Jack thought about the fact that Rose did not know about the Field Generator Weapon. He walked over to the War Room and prayed for Holy isolation again. He told Mark, Laura, Sarah, and Alexis about what had just transpired. "Don't mention anything about the FG stuff to anyone outside of this meeting until after the battle tomorrow, understand?"

# CHAPTER THIRTY-SIX

Jack had heard from Rose that Satan had accepted the change to the original deal. He marveled at his own boldness as he walked out onto the deserted aft deck of the luxury liner just before noon local time.

He prayed that Yahshua would guide his actions in this affair. Jack checked that his Field Generator's light was green. It was a beautiful sunny and warm day off of the Israeli coast and it seemed almost tranquil. Then an ugly as sin demon stalked onto the deck carrying a big black sword. It spied Jack and charged him with its sword on high. Jack had figured that there would be some form of a preliminary battle to put him at ease before the main match with Xndalius. He prayed intently to God and his armor and sword flashed into sight as he met the charge of the demon. The big black blade shattered against the bright chrome blade with the essence of Yahveh flowing off its length. Jack spun to his left and decapitated the demon with one blow. He stepped back as the stinky body slowly collapsed to the deck and evaporated into demon stain. Jack twirled his blade and resheathed it.

He heard Satan chuckle. "Don't get too comfortable General Malone. Now, you will meet my champion and die."

The new demon that stalked onto the deck was even larger than the first one. This one was very confident and glided toward Jack across the deck with murder in its eyes. As they met with a crash Jack had his sword casually knocked aside and Xndalius backhanded his larger sword to cut Jack's head from his body. The blade hit the protection field of the Field Generator and stopped. Jack took his opportunity and slammed his blade into the demon's side only to see it slide off Xndalius' armor. The two combatants exchanged five more blows each with no damage to either man or demon. Xndalius whirled into a furious assault attempting to batter Jack to the ground without effect.

Jack reached up and pushed the blue switch on his body armor and sensed an enormous level of power come into play. He focused on Xndalius and spoke the power words. **"In the name and by the authority of Yahveh God, I destroy this single creature!"**

Jack saw the full understanding flare into the demon's eyes as he spoke those fateful words. But, it was too late for Xndalius. The demon shattered into a thousand fragments as it was consumed from the inside out by a power so bright it shined brighter than the sun. In less than a split second Xndalius disappeared totally and the deck of the luxury liner went totally silent as all creation stood in awe of the demon's destruction. Jack's armor and sword faded from view as every demon for miles, including Satan, fled in great fear. Carefully switching off the blue switch Jack sensed a feeling of relief.

Jack sank to his knees and prayed his thanks to Yahveh God in the name of His Son, Yahshua. Then Jack prayed that God would take this "weapon" away from him. He heard the Father say, *"I have removed this weapon capability from you for now. Until I have need of it again."*

Jack thanked God from a full heart of love. He stood up and switched off his Field Generator and he was very aware of the fact that the blue switch simply wasn't there anymore.

There was a major celebration on the Sword that evening for the successful completion of this new level of battle with the demonic forces of darkness.

Mark watched the videos of Jack's battle with the Archdemon Xndalius in satisfaction knowing that this whole event was the Father's way of reminding Satan and the world of the demonic that He was God. "WOW"!

In Heaven Rose had watched the battle with the knowledge that Jack had dedicated everything to the Most High and win or lose, his place in Heaven was assured by the atoning death and resurrection of Yahshua, his Messiah. But the stunning victory and destruction of their ages old enemy Xndalius at the elemental, no, at the nuclear sub-atomic level so lifted her heart she exalted the name of God throughout the Heavens. Her small part in helping to encourage Jack prior to the battle had been crucial to his strength to actually use God's power and his desire to step away from it once he had used it. She was very happy for him and the rest of the Crossfire Team.

Raquel met with Raziel and they celebrated with the Heavenly Host because the Most High had found a human truly worth His investment of power to destroy the ugliness that had been Xndalius.

Jack had stepped out on the flying bridge of the Sword that was sailing west into the Atlantic Ocean and he thrilled to everything God was doing, and had done since before time began. His own spirit was full of joy and he was actually looking forward to his future and that of everyone that was a part of the team.

He was joined by Hugh Kelly on the small wing station outside of the bridge of the ship. The XO quietly shared in Jack's victory for a while and then spoke. "Nice piece of work there, General. I have an event facing us that I would like your advice on."

Jack looked the XO, "How can I be of service, Commander Kelly?"

Hugh smiled, "It seems that China has become interested in the Sword since we used their base to fend off our American submarine shadows and are actively seeking us to satisfy that interest. The American CIA and the Mossad have notified us that the Chinese Government has recently devoted a sizable portion of their funds and naval resources to the singular goal of capturing this ship and acquiring its capabilities and potential for warfare. How do you think we should proceed in discouraging this desire of theirs?"

Jack had been silently praying for God's input on this matter as Hugh explained it. He smiled, "I think we need to present the requirement that the entire Nation of China must embrace Yahshua and Judeo-Christianity before they seek to use God's resources."

Hugh nodded his head. "I agree with that requirement. How do we send them that message?"

Jack grinned, "No sending involved, I think God wants us to take the word to them in person."

# CHAPTER THIRTY-SEVEN

Jack called a Core Team meeting to present this new concept to them for their consideration. "I want to do this piece of "world level diplomacy" God's way and not "our" way. So, I'm going to pray for the Core team to hear from the Father on how He wants us to "explain" to the Chinese Security Premier why it is futile for them to pursue us or attempt to "get" our "technology" from us, our ship, Force Generators, or aircraft."

Jack began to pray. "Yahshua, this action places us where you said we were not anointed to go. Yet, this "courtesy" call on the Chinese Premier could eliminate a great deal of warfare between that country and us. If You do not want us to interface with the Premier and prefer to handle this Yourself, let us know so that we do not go against You in our effort to prevent unnecessary death and destruction. Show us Your Will."

The Son of God's communion with each person on the Core Team was intense and enriching. After a while Jack stood up and called everyone to attention. "All right, assuming that each of you has heard from the Savior, let us take a vote. Does God want us to make a visit in His Name to China or do we not get involved that way?"

The vote was unanimous for them to go to China, not as the Crossfire Team, but, as emissaries of. Which one would expect if everyone truly heard from Heaven.

Jack smiled, "All right, now we need to understand exactly what we must do and what we must not do according to God. I want each of you to enter into your workstation the twenty most important directions you got from the Father and send them to Ethan's workstation so he can collate and prioritize them. Get started."

Jack also wrote out his list and submitted it to Ethan Reaper. After twenty minutes Ethan posted the combined list and it was very close to what each person had listed.

Jack picked the first ten items in order:

1. Make an appointment to speak to the Chinese Premier soon

2.  Take no more than five people
3.  Each person must wear an active Field Generator
4.  Present a simple explanation that spells out our relationship to God and His Kingdom
5.  Explain our charter against the Demonic and Satan not against non-aggressive human organizations, regimes, or governments
6.  Offer to remain neutral with China if possible
7.  Don't get involved with politics or military issues
8.  Refer all requests to God
9.  Avoid releasing any information about, or descriptions of, our capabilities
10. Avoid confrontational statements or threats

Jack nodded his head after reading the list. "Which five people should go? I am going to suggest five men because the Chinese are still a male dominated society and will be more likely to listen to men. As leaders I am going to suggest myself, Mark, and David. For communications Ethan Reaper, and as the most knowledgeable of the society, language, and politics, I suggest Charlie Wu. Any thoughts or substitutions anyone would like to recommend?"

No one spoke up and the planning for the trip began. Jack placed a coded call to a special cell phone deep within China. Zhou Tangtao responded very quickly to the call. This was a very dangerous thing for the powerful

Vice-Premier of the Chinese Government Security Powers to do. "Jack, in the Holy Name of Yahshua how are you, Laura, Mark and the others doing in your battles with the enemy?"

Jack smiled, "Shalom, Zhou, in the Name of Yahshua HaMashiach. We are all well and pray for you and your family daily. I'll make this quick. I'm sure you are aware of your government's new quest to acquire our ship and or our technology. It is not ours to give away. It is God's power. We are going to attempt to have a sit down to explain this to your Premier. What do think of our chances to see him and to convince him that neither China nor any other government can possess these powers?"

Zhou considered everything and then laughed quietly. "Jack, you will probably get an audience with the Premier but I would think it will be a trap and the security forces will attempt to restrain you and anything you come here on. He cannot make agreement to not try and possess your technology and stay in power. Are you sure you want to meet with him?"

Jack laughed with Zhou. "Yes, it is God's plan to display our capability without having to kill a lot of your troops. We will be safe and will leave when we want to leave. It will probably be smart for you to not be involved unless the Father tells you to do it."

Zhou agreed and thanked Jack for the heads up. He broke the connection.

Jack had Ethan set up a call to the Chinese State Department and he politely asked for a meeting with the Premier as soon as possible. They told him that they would be in touch.

Mark agreed that they would want to meet due to the Chinese desire to own the Crossfire Team's technology.

Four hours later the American State Department called Jack. "Mr. Malone, we are interested in your application to meet the Premier of China. Personally, I'd like to know the reason for the meeting and why you would do this as a private citizen rather than coordinate through us."

Jack prayed for God's words since they weren't supposed to acting on the world stage at this level. He was surprised by the response he got from Heaven. "I'm sorry. I did not get your name. So, Sir, the meeting is a private one between my team and China. I did not check with you first because we are no longer American citizens. I am officially an Israeli citizen and am not in your coverage zone anymore. And, before you ask, my government knows about the meeting and has approved it as a personal matter. Please, have a nice day."

Jack broke the connection and looked at Laura's raised eyebrow and grinned. "I've wanted to do that for a long time."

Laura nodded her head. "Jack that statement would have a lot more meaning if I knew who you were talking to, don't you think?"

Jack shrugged, "That was a no-namer from the American State Department wanting me to grant him authority to tell me what I can and cannot do in regards to our China trip."

Laura thought that through and smiled. "Then I would say, "Good call"."

Ethan called Jack, "You've got another call from the U.S. State Department. Do you want to talk to them again?"

Jack said "Sure, hook me up Ethan."

A different voice was on the line. "Mr. Malone? My name is Henry J. Walker and I am the U. S. Under Secretary of State. I understand one of my staffers called you and acted improperly. I would like to apologize for his actions."

Jack responded, "Thank you Mr. Secretary, I appreciate the apology. I believe I gave that young man the particulars on my upcoming visit to meet with the Chinese Premier. Including the fact that it is a personal visit that doesn't involve the United States. I am no longer an American citizen and I doubt that America will even come up in my meeting. Does the State Department understand my position on this?"

Mr. Walker didn't sound upset or concerned. "We do understand your position and thank you for your time."

The Secretary broke the connection and Jack grinned. "Now, _he is_ a good statesman. He sounded uninterested in my meeting and didn't dig for information. That tells me that State is probably already seeking White House authority for escalating their need to know why and what will be discussed in China."

Mark had been listening to the conversations. "If that's the case, you can bet dollars to donuts that a dozen different "friendly" nations want to know too. Plus, another dozen "unfriendly" nations that really want in on this trip."

David chimed in, "Yeah, but the most telling Intel from State's calls is that we are going to get our meeting and the Chinese haven't even asked us what we want to talk about, yet."

Laura had been silently praying and made the audible statement to no one in particular, "You tell him."

Mark smiled, "I think you need to check with God."

Jack bowed his head and began to worship the Creator of the Universe when he stopped talking and obviously went to "Receive".

A minute later he looked up at Mark. "The Father gave me an update on our trip. Laura, Sarah, Alexis, Christi, and Linda Wu will be accompanying the five of us to China as is customary for visiting heads of state."

Mark shrugged his shoulders, "Okay, but why? We, you, aren't heads of state. Possibly head of ship, but, state?"

Jack nodded, "Doesn't matter, Yahveh wants them there for His reasons. End of debate."

# CHAPTER THIRTY-EIGHT

The ten travelers met separately after the Core Team meeting. Jack looked at his wife closely. "Laura, I know you well enough to know that you wouldn't ask God to intercede for the females of this group to go on the China trip. Did the Father give you a special reason for the five women to make the trip?"

Laura was actually impressed that Jack knew there was more to the girls going to China than a sightseeing jaunt. She smiled, "There is a definite reason God wants us on this trip. I have nothing I can share with you yet beyond the fact He has an unstated purpose for us to be there."

Jack nodded, "Okay then, we will not organize an itinerary for you guys. Obviously, stay in touch with us by our new CrayCom link." Ethan had worked with Crayton to create a new, ultra-secure communications link for the team. The communication algorithms were changing constantly every picosecond on both ends of the link and only the team computers could unscramble the signals.

Jack handed out a package of papers to each person in the room. He told everyone to memorize the information in the packets and then destroy the packets. He dismissed everyone except Laura, Ethan, and Christi.

When they were alone Jack smiled at the two newer members to set their minds at ease. "I want to let you two guys know that you are both going on this trip as unattached single members and not acting like a fifth couple. At least for this trip I want you two to back each other up when the need arises and work with everyone else like normal.

Jack nodded and dismissed them. They parted ways as friends and fellow warriors.

The next morning the "Sword" neared the Chinese coast and responded to the usual challenge with the information concerning the Premier's invitation. The naval authority instructed the Sword to a sheltered dock at the somewhat secret naval base they had approached. The ten-person party left the ship and was taken to an airbase where a passenger aircraft and two limousines awaited them to take them to the Premier's residence in Beijing.

Since Jack could speak Chinese in several dialects including High Mandarin. He introduced the men in his party and those with the premier. Jack then turned the presentation over to Charlie Wu.

Charlie used some honorifics to establish the Premier's position at the meeting. This honored the Premier and showed the team's respect for his lofty position in China. Charlie then explained the team's role as servants of God. This was a foreign concept in the Atheistic nation of China. The ex-Chinese spy then apologetically explained that the weapons that the team used were protected by God Himself and in point of fact were powered by God to allow the team to battle the legions of demons from Satan's demonic realm. The team was not involved in national politics and had no agenda to interfere with the Chinese and their political goals.

Jack had carefully listened to Charlie's presentation and watched the faces of the ruling group. Orientals may not show a great deal of reaction but their body language spoke volumes about what they thought. Jack could see a lot of dissatisfaction and disbelief after the presentation.

The Premier consulted with his people and came to a conclusion. He addressed Jack directly in high Mandarin. "Mr. Malone, even though we are somewhat at a loss in dealing with the concept of an ultimate entity that directs and empowers his followers, we still have to survive in the world by dealing with people we can see, touch, and interface with on a daily basis. The fact that your "Sword" ship can ram a destroyer and totally annihilate it without any damage to your vessel is a worldly fact and we mean to have that capability for our ships. Any other course of action would be folly. What price do you require for the secrets of your ship?"

This was roughly what the team had expected. Jack carefully set the tone for any negotiations. "While we thank you for what is surely a generous offer, we cannot give you what is not ours to give as Mr. Wu explained earlier. No man has designed the weapons systems that protect us in battle. These are strictly a gift from God. As was explained we have no agenda for or against China or America, or any other nation including Israel. We came here openly and honestly to work cooperatively with your nation much as we do with the nation of Israel today. This would be to both of our advantages." Jack sat down to await the Premier's answer.

Again the Premier consulted with his people. Afterward the Premier got up and left the area. A Chinese Admiral addressed Jack directly. "Mr. Malone, by direct order of the Premier I am placing you and your men here under arrest for conspiring against the nation of China, I am also placing the rest of your ship's crew under arrest and am impounding your ship. You and your people are being considered as terrorists and therefore have no rights whatsoever and you are not entitled to legal representation at this time. Do you understand what I have told you?"

As the Admiral had been talking thirty Chinese Special Forces types with automatic weapons had quietly surrounded the team.

Jack did not stand up since the ambush clearly showed a total lack of honesty in the Chinese dealings. "Admiral, I understand what you say, but I do not accept your authority in these matters and reject your intention to arrest any of my people or impound our ship. While we are offended by the actions of your government we will return to our ship and return to our business. My advice to you is that any attempt to keep us from leaving is useless and any damages, injuries, or deaths involved in your efforts to illegally detain us or our ship are completely on your head. You have been warned."

Jack picked up his brief case and rose from his seat along with the other four team members. Mark commented, "Dang, I sometimes wish we couldn't predict so precisely how these consultations will go."

The Chinese troops aimed their weapons at the team members and threatened to shoot them if they didn't surrender.

The five team members ignored the troops completely and continued to walk out of the room. Not really wanting to kill the men; several troops slung their weapons and tried to restrain Jack. Jack simply kept walking and the troops could not get any purchase on him. Several troops locked arms and blocked Jack's path. Jack met the resistance and thought his way along the corridor. The Force Generator used only sufficient force to allow Jack to proceed at his pace.

By now the team members and the troops exited the residence and approached a parking lot. The exasperated troops finally stepped back and fired their automatic weapons at the team members. The bullets never reached the team; Mark nodded as they reached the spot where the limos were. There were no vehicles present. Mark spoke into his CrayCom link and a Fragment dropped out of the skies and came to rest in front of the Crossfire Team. The five men walked up the stairs in a hail of bullets and closed the hatch. By the time they had sat down the Fragment took only three minutes to arrive at the Sword and was quickly lowered into the hull. Ten minutes later the five men met Captain Conners on the bridge.

# CHAPTER THIRTY-NINE

Captain Conners shook Jack's hand. "Well, that pretty well went exactly as you thought it would. As for our sailing away, the Chinese have gotten a little creative here. He pointed at one screen. They have not only parked a WWII Battleship completely behind us sideward to our only departure path, but they scuttled it too. It's sitting on the bottom of the bay."

Ethan stared at for a few seconds. "Man, that must be one tall ship! It still towers above us even though it's on the bottom." He looked at Jack, "What about your wives and Christi?"

Jack grinned, "I think they are shopping. We'll send a plane to get them after we ease out of this little parking problem."

Jack turned to Hugh Kelly, "Well, XO, have you been practicing your FG forced maneuvers?"

Hugh shook his head slightly. "Yes General, I have. Let's see what I can do here. Do we want to warn the Chinese to vacate the area first?"

Jack nodded his head. Hugh put a call into the Naval Yard's Port Master. "Please have no personnel anywhere on the scuttled ship behind us or anywhere within a quarter mile on either side of a line directly to our stern. This will be your one and only warning."

Hugh watched and saw no personnel or movement in the described area. "Right then." He signaled for maneuvering power astern. As the stern of the Sword neared the old ship in their way, Hugh visualized that ship being moved out of their way.

When the Huge FG field on the Sword reached the scuttled Battleship, it was slapped away from their path. It looked like a giant, invisible fist punched the old battlewagon in the side facing the Sword. That "punch" broke the armored hull, folded the eight-hundred-foot long ship in half and knocked it a thousand yards away from the Sword, completely clearing a sufficient path allowing the Sword's departure. As the Sword sailed calmly away from its mooring, dozens of shell-shocked dock workers staggered out of their barracks to stare with great awe at what just a little touch of God's finger could accomplish.

As they sailed away from the harbor a flight of Chinese war planes strafed and bombed the Sword without any effect or retaliation.

Jack called Laura on the CrayCom link and told her of the meeting and the aftermath at the harbor. Laura said that the atmosphere had recently turned much cooler than at first and they felt it was probably a good time to come home.

Jack was going to send a Fragment but Laura suggested that Rob bring the Formidable instead.

As soon as the men walked out of their meeting with the Premier, Laura knew that the Internal Security would come for them. She knew because it was a logical result of their being unable to stop the men. She also knew because the Father wanted to use the Chinese belief that men were somehow more important than women. God wanted to make a statement that equality is preferred by Him. Apparently, it was up to the women to make a positive statement that would bring praise to the Father and the Son. Looking at a bevy of fawning female clerks and sales personnel Laura asked Sarah, "How unbalanced are the odds now?"

Sarah had been keeping an eye on the internal security forces along with Linda Wu who once was one of those forces. Linda said in a soft, barely heard voice, "There are three armored personnel carriers out front and probably three more out back. That means that they will move very soon. How do you want to handle it when they do?"

Sarah laughed quietly, "We've all got our FGs on so they can't do anything to us, but, that doesn't mean they won't try to intimidate us by threatening to hurt other people."

Alexis looked mad, "They really don't want to do that!"

Suddenly the sales staff and the local customers quickly left the store. In the resulting quiet Christi said, "Show Time."

Three Internal Security Agents walked over to the five women and identified themselves. They insisted that the five Western women accompany them downtown to answer some questions. Laura looked at her watch and smiled at the three agents. "I'm really sorry, but we can't go with you. You see, we're due back on our ship in a few minutes."

The lead agent was a rail thin man who raised his right hand and snapped his fingers. Twenty Special Forces troops rushed into the store and quickly surrounded the five women. The agent said, in very good English, "And I'm afraid that you are not going back to your ship. You will go with me as I asked you to do before."

Laura had suffered all the male dominance attitude she wanted to at that point. "Understand this! You and all your forces have neither the authority nor the ability to tell us what to do. Now, back off or suffer some very embarrassing actions on your part."

The agent was not about to let a mere woman speak to him in this manner. He attempted to slap her in the face which did not work like he planned. His hand was moving with sufficient force to hurt her somewhat, definitely redden her face when he felt like he had slapped the side of the building instead. His hand and wrist screamed in pain and the object of his instruction was standing there, unhurt and unamused. She reached out with her left hand and simply slapped him back. The difference was that his head snapped to the side and the slap threw him off his feet to the floor. Not only was his face red, but he also had a broken jaw and had lost several teeth in the exchange. Grabbing his face, he told his men to shoot her. The guards got away with four shots which rang out quickly before Sarah and Christi disarmed the shooters and rendered them unconscious.

Laura shook her head and told her teammates, "Let's go ladies; I am tired of talking to morons who will not listen, in any language."

The five women took their purchases outside and waited for Rob. Sarah heard it first and looked up. Rob used their pendants to home in on and lowered the Formidable to the street directly in front of them. As they proceeded to enter the craft two of the APCs fired their 28mm cannons at the plane. There was no appreciable damage to the women or the plane, but several dozens of bystanders were injured in the crowd which had stampeded to flee the canon fire. This action irritated Christi and Alexis enough that they handed their purchases to Sarah and walked with determination directly at the two twenty-ton vehicles.

Before the soldiers in the APCs could decide what to do, the women reached the vehicles. Alexis watched the cannon on her APC rotate to point at her with the end of the muzzle only inches from her face. She made a fist with her right hand and shoved it into the barrel of the cannon which was immediately fired. She had hoped that by stopping up the barrel the explosion would shatter the cannon barrel. Instead, the Field Generator absorbed the energy and the projectile slid out of the barrel and fell out of the barrel after Alexis took her hand out. The projectile fell straight down where the nose struck the ground at Alexis' feet. And, then it exploded.

The force of the exploding cannon round didn't affect Alexis but it did blow the front of the APC into the air high enough to flip the vehicle over onto its back. Alexis smiled, that put it out of service and it no longer poised a threat to the innocents around it.

Christi walked up to the APC on her side of the action just as it fired its cannon directly at her. Christi thought that was just rude and concentrated and thought the vehicle out of her path. The field around Christi slammed the APC eighty feet away and into a large, unused, brick building. The violence of the APC smashing through the main wall on the first floor caused the other four stories to collapse onto the APC, effectively putting it out of action.

The two women walked back to the plane and boarded it. Rob gently lifted the Formidable up and away from the street scene and flew back to the Sword.

Jack summed the whole mission up as a learning lesson for everyone. But, he told Laura when they were alone that he had an unsettled feeling in his spirit and was concerned that the trip may have simply intrigued the Chinese even more. He recalled when a rogue member of the ruling government went after the Team's family and associates in an attempt to control the team.

Laura agreed somewhat but had a different concern. "We know God sees all things from the end to the beginning, right? We also know that he is never wrong. Well then, He approved this mission knowing it would not really deter the Chinese but could fascinate them even more. Why? What does our Father want by increasing their interest in our capability? I wonder if He isn't setting the stage to show that country of roughly two billion people that He is God and to compete they need His help. We may just be the unattainable jewel that drives them to realize they need God on their side after all.

Jack thought that over and decided that they needed to be the most unattainable jewel the Chinese had ever wanted.

# CHAPTER FORTY

David, Mark, and Sarah were sitting with Jack after they had been sailing for more than six hours in international waters. They were discussing the probable reactions from the Chinese toward the team.

David commented on the Chinese mindset. "Once they publically set their sights on something they then feel honor-bound to achieve, acquire, or possess the object of their interest. It becomes like goal of the group, organization, or public interested in the object. It becomes "theirs" because they desire it. Actually it is similar to how many thieves function. If you have a valuable item, say a watch, which they want, in their mind it becomes theirs and you are preventing them from having what is "theirs". That makes it acceptable to steal it because it is really theirs, not yours. Now, I'm not saying the Chinese think that way but the actions are similar."

Mark nodded his head. "That is true in essence in this case. They want it and will do, pay, or accomplish anything to get it. Our situation is different in that we don't own or possess the powers involved and they can't steal them from us. But, I believe they will try to coerce us into giving them the secret to the power. I think it would take God to change their minds."

Jack nodded. "This "desire" of theirs is going to lead to conflict between us before it is resolved. We peacefully went to them and explained these things to them and they refused to believe us. So we demonstrated their inability to capture or hurt us. Still they seem determined to have this "power". I agree with Mark that we need to give the problem to God."

Everyone else agreed and Jack bowed his head and began to pray. As soon as he started he sensed a change in location and opened his eyes. He beheld a glorious sight. The four of them were in Heaven in a mansion-like setting with color beyond description and beauty everywhere they looked. The Angel Rose appeared in front of them and smiled. "Welcome warriors of the Crossfire Team. The Most

High wants to answer your prayer of concern about the Chinese and the power He provides you. Now hear the Word of the Lord." *"My faithful warriors, I understand your concern about these people. I will use you as an example of a blessed life in me not the fearful life in the world. Ignore their attempts to engage you in battle and rise above their way of life. Deep down they still know that honor is the true mark of a man or woman. If their attempts to engage you threaten innocent lives, prevent that as necessary regardless of their losses. Otherwise deal with these people in love as My Son would, in all things. You shall be My example."*

Rose smiled at the four people and whirled out of sight in a flurry of bright white and gold.

Mark held up his hands. "There you go; we have our direction for the Chinese problem. Any questions?"

Jack asked, "Why are we still here? I like it but why?"

Sarah looked at Jack. "Because God is not done with us yet. I sincerely doubt that He forgot to send us back."

That made sense to everyone so they waited quietly. Jack got up and walked over to a door and opened it. The beauty and fantastic vistas went on in all directions. Jack turned around, "Let's take a walk."

The other three joined him and they moved through the area next to the building they had been in. Everything was so peaceful and soothing to the soul. After a while they came to a man standing by a river. Jack greeted the man and asked if he knew where they should go. The man looked at the four of them and smiled. He raised his right arm and pointed to a building on a hill about a half of a mile distant. His voice was melodic and caring. "That is where you want to go, Jack."

Jack looked at the man, "Do we know each other?" "We did at one time." He held out his hand to shake

Jack's. "Alan Throman, your first Pastor."

Jack was astonished as were Mark and Sarah. "Alan! I'm so glad to see you. We've missed you."

"And I've missed all of you also. How is your delightful wife, Laura?"

"She's fine and will be sad to have missed you."

The man smiled, "Tell her not to worry, we will have eternity to talk after you get here. But, I'm being a little remiss here, you need to go to that building, it has been wonderful seeing you all." He waved goodbye as they moved on.

They quickly reached the large building and entered the large front door. Hugo was sitting in a comfortable chair and waved them over. He rose as they drew near. "The Father wanted you to get a taste of Heaven and to fulfill Alan's wish to see you. I am pleased you enjoyed your time. We will meet again very soon." Hugo faded out of sight and they found themselves back in the War Room on the Sword.

# CHAPTER FORTY-ONE

Laura was sitting there watching them. "Welcome back, how was your trip?"

Jack got up, walked over and leaned down and kissed her on the cheek. "Exceptional, different and we met an old friend, Alan Throman. He told me to wish you well and said that we will have lots of time to talk later. Interestingly, Hugo told us that one reason we went to Heaven was because Alan wished to see us."

Laura was smiling, "How did he look? Did you know him?"

Jack laughed, "Not at all, He was about thirty years old and looking very hale and hardy. He's just as humble and polite as ever. After he identified himself I recognized his voice and demeanor."

Laura laughed, "I'm glad he was there. I take you had other business there also."

Mark spoke up, "Yes we did. We've got God's marching orders on how to deal with the Chinese interest in us. Essentially, we ignore them unless innocents are in jeopardy then we end it so no one gets hurt except the Chinese. Otherwise we are to act like Christ as an example to them."

Sarah said, "God said "My faithful warriors, I understand your concern about these people. I will use you as an example of a blessed life in me, not the fearful life in the world. Ignore their attempts to engage you in battle and rise above their way of life. Deep down they still know that honor is the true mark of a man or woman. If their attempts to engage you threaten innocent lives, prevent that as necessary regardless of their losses. Otherwise deal with these people in love as My Son would, in all things. You shall be My example."

She grinned, "I've wanted to do that for a while. When the Father speaks it stays in my mind, word for word."

The phone rang and Laura answered it. She handed it to Jack. He listened for several minutes and said, "Yes Sir."

He pointed at Mark, "We're needed on the bridge right away."

When they walked onto the bridge they met Captain Conners. He motioned them over to the plot board. "Gentlemen, we have a situation and need to make a decision. He pointed to the indicator of their position on the display. Then he pointed to another indicator nearby that was flashing red. We're eighteen miles south, southwest of the Cruise ship "Dream Tide" flagged out of Singapore. They are broadcasting a Mayday signal that they are being threatened by pirates. It is an unwritten rule that any ship within range respond to a Mayday signal. I'm thinking we are in unchartered waters here. I find it strange that we bust out of a Chinese military port and within twelve hours we are presented with an emergency on a Chinese liner. How do you want to handle it?"

Jack smiled, "What would Yahshua do? I suggest we treat the emergency as a real one and offer to assist. If it is a Chinese machination, we'll deal with them at that point. Captain, make all speed to the vicinity of the Mayday. XO, determine how we can assist. We're certainly well-armed enough to repel pirates if needed."

The Sword turned to a north by northwest heading and submerged. The ship increased speed to two hundred knots and quickly closed the distance to the Chinese liner.

The XO, Hugh Kelly handled the operation as a seasoned pirate fighter. He had been through four different assaults on pirates preying on international shipping. This was a first time with a cruise liner with so many hostages though.

Mark recalled his action with the Israeli Cruise Ship and wondered if this would be similar.

Hugh sighed, "It seems the pirates have already boarded the liner because she is stopped and there are four small boats tied up on the leeward side. He brought the Sword to a full stop.

Hugh called out and order. "Comm, hail the liner and let's see what this band of nutcases are demanding."

It seemed that the pirates were demanding fifty million dollars American and freedom to depart or they would start killing hostages in one hour.

Mark said, "We're being herded. No one demands that kind of money with a one-hour deadline. It would never happen.

Jack shook his head. "We don't have any information on the number of terrorists, who they are, or who they think they think they are negotiating with. Captain, tell them it will take roughly twenty-four hours to raise that kind of cash. Mark, let's pray about this and then go invisible, go over there, and kill all the pirates starting with the leaders.

Mark nodded, "My kind of plan."

Prayer encouraged Jack's plan and twenty warriors slid out of the vehicle lock and approached the liner swimming invisibly on the surface.

Climbing on-board using the pirate's ladders the men and women spread through the ship. Jack and Mark took the bridge. Finding the leader there with the Captain something didn't look right. They were talking together more like friends and there was no sign of weapon being brandished or fear. The others checked in with no sign of pirates or interruption of routines.

Jack said, "Hmmm, I don't think this is a hostile takeover."

Mark said "Probably not, but I don't speak Chinese."

Jack nodded, "I do, stand down the troops and let me listen to these two for a few minutes."

It took all of two minutes to confirm that this Mayday was just a ruse to lure the Crossfire Team. Jack thought for a minute, prayed for a minute and then told Mark to become visible. Jack and Mark appeared with their silenced weapons pointed at both men. To say they were surprised would have been an understatement.

Jack said in Chinese, "Bang, you're dead! If this had been an actual pirate attack all of your men would have died quietly and without warning. As it is, we need to hold you both for the authorities for initiating a false Mayday call."

The Captain shook his head. "That would make you look foolish. We only generated a Mayday signal that your ship could receive. We would deny doing it.

Jack asked, "We have recorded the call and can easily prove you sent it. Then you would be guilty and liars.

Why would you do that?"

"Our intention was to lure you here."

"As I asked, "Why"

The supposed Pirate leader smiled, "To attempt to analyze the technology of you and your ship."

Mark chuckled, "Do your sensors work in the supernatural spectrum?"

Jack used the CommNet "All troops, bad Intel, return to the Sword immediately.

He and Mark turned to walk out and a small Chinese man aimed an unknown weapon at them and triggered it. It hummed and emitted a blue beam which didn't affect either man. They disappeared and returned to their ship.

Jack muttered "Show them the love of Yahshua; Show them the love of Yahshua."

# CHAPTER FORTY-TWO

As the Sword left the area around the Chinese liner Jack looked at Mark, "Somehow I think that little stunt is going to boomerang on them someday."

Jack called the Captain. "Captain Conners, can you shake the Chinese off of our backs?"

"I think so. I'll let you know."

The Sword left the liner and disappeared from sight and from sonar as it sank below the water and faded out. The submerged speed rose to over two hundred knots for the next hour. The Sword came to a halt and the advanced sensors scanned air, surface, and under water with no contacts anywhere. The Captain called Jack and confirmed that they had lost the Chinese sub that had been tracking them.

Jack smiled, "Don't think that they will give up trying to track us. Maybe we should slide through some areas near U.S. bases. We are possibly less noticeable than they are and they'll have to avoid places like that."

Captain Conners concurred and signed off. Jack put the Chinese out of his mind and concentrated on other avenues of pressure that could be brought against the team members. Friends, family members, businesses, and things like that. For his own family the only members the Chinese would find were his wife who was with him, his mom and dad who were living in Israel under assumed names along with his Uncle Larry in Tel Aviv and protected by the Mossad and especially by Iris Jakobson, the Director of the Mossad. They were very busy integrating the Jewish way of life into their lives.

Jack called Laura and together they prayed for God's guidance concerning the Chinese efforts to appropriate God's power for themselves. After a while they were worshipping Yahveh when they sensed a presence. Opening their eyes, they beheld the Archangel Raquel surrounded by some form of great power radiating around and away from him. He saw them and seemed to step out of everything into their presence. "Hello Jack and Laura, Yes, I'm here in response to your prayers."

Jack squeezed Laura's hand, "Hello Raquel. Thank you for coming to help us resolve our concern."

Jack and Laura sat on the bed. Laura asked "What do we do from God's perspective?"

Raquel nodded his head, "Several specific things and a general recommendation. First thing is to "change your "attitude" in response to their harassment of your operations. You know how important your work is for God's Kingdom and they need to respect what you do, regardless of their beliefs. Yes, the Most High wants you to treat them as Yahshua would when He was on Earth. But, He never let men interfere in His work for the Kingdom. You, likewise should admonish the Chinese efforts to meddle in your affairs. Do this gently at first, then with increasing firmness until they acquiesce to your requests."

"Secondly, they will never find a way to equal any of God's tools He has given to you. God will confound their efforts and limit their intelligence in this area. Regardless of their pronouncements they will not succeed. Your use of God's power will forever escape them until they humble themselves and reach out to God."

"One of their efforts will be using the occult as they did in the far past. God will allow this effort to proceed until they conjure up something they can't control. They will be frightened and will contact you for help. This will be an honest plea for help and you need to help them."

"In general, the Chinese effort will attract the attention of Marco Marino in his efforts to eliminate your team. This will not affect you but will cause strife between the Chinese and the Anti-Christ that will ease his preoccupation with you."

Jack nodded, Thank you Raquel. We appreciate you and your efforts on our behalf."

The Archangel smiled and faded out of sight.

Laura sighed, "So, we will have to contend with the Chinese efforts for a while longer. How do you feel about that?"

Jack pulled her close to him, "We can handle their efforts, especially now that we know they will not succeed."

She snuggled into his embrace. "That's good, I am ready for some quiet time for a bit. You know, time to reconnect, and time to recharge our batteries." She kissed his cheek. He kissed her and pulled her closer.

# CHAPTER FORTY-THREE

Things were actually pretty quiet for the next six days. On the morning of the seventh day, ComSec received an open message for the Crossfire Team from an Admiral of the Chinese Northern Fleet. In short form the message said that the Chinese had a maverick Captain that seemed to be possessed by evil spirits who was determined to take his ship into a U.S. Naval Base and use tactical nuclear weapons in revenge for the atom bomb attacks on Japan in WWII.

They had been unable to stop him or change his mind. There was less than ten hours until he was in range to launch his weapons. Also, their attempts to board his ship were repelled by an indestructible force.

Jack looked at Mark. "What do you think? Is it another Red Herring?"

Mark shook his head, "I'm not sure, they could have gotten those symptoms from records of our previous actions. I think we need Heavenly advice on this."

Jack spoke, "Raquel".

The Archangel appeared, "Yes, Jack".

Jack reviewed the previous ruse and asked if this Mayday was another one like it.

Raquel smiled, "I will see." He disappeared.

He came back in ten minutes. "This call was true, there were demons running the Captain and the ship."

Mark asked, "There *were* demons, as in, they not there now?"

Raquel nodded his head, "It seemed my presence frightened them so much that they fled back into their dimension and the Captain realized his folly and turned control over to his second in command who reversed direction and is now steaming away from the U.S. Base."

Jack walked over and shook the Archangel's hand. "Thank you Raquel. Again, we really appreciate your efforts in resolving this matter."

Raquel smiled, "You are very welcome. I'm glad I could be of assistance." He then faded out of sight.

Mark had Ethan send a message to the Chinese Admiral advising him that the situation had been remedied."

Not soon afterward the Admiral sent back an inquiry as to how they had handled the evil spirits. Mark replied that they had Heavenly help in dispatching the evil spirits.

Later that day the Admiral asked if he and an aide could visit them to discuss the earlier situation. Mark and Jack took the request to Captain Conners.

When they met in the Captain's quarters Mark asked, "Can we allow them access to the Sword without giving away anything we shouldn't?"

The Captain thought about that for a few minutes. "Yes, I believe we could entertain visitors as long as we don't give them a tour of the ship. There is really nothing they can deduce from simply being here. Try to remember that we really *are* powered and protected by God and they will never duplicate that in any manner."

Jack agreed to the visit and met the Admiral and his Aide and took them to the War Room to sit down and talk.

Admiral Zhang Wei was impressed by the big ship and its smoothness through the sea but was truly focused on the problem of the errant Captain.

Jack tried to explain the supernatural world to the man but he just could not truly believe in spirits. "General Malone, do you actually expect me to believe in other worldly beings that I cannot see or touch which can enter our world and interfere in our operations?"

Jack smiled at the Admiral, "That is the truth and the reality that we deal with every day, Admiral."

The Admiral liked Jack and didn't want to feel that Jack was trying to pull something over on him. But, in his whole life he had never seen anything to convince him that this spirit world existed. He was about to criticize this line of reasoning when a deep voice from behind him made him turn around.

The Angel Caleb stood there. "Admiral Zhang Wei, the Most High God wants you to truly understand the reality of the universe. You are not alone as a species in the universe. I am an Angel of God almighty. You can see me." Caleb reached out and touched the Admirals arm. "You can touch me. I am a messenger of the Most High God. The age of the Gentiles has come to an end and the age of the Messiah has begun. The question I have for you is, will you bow your head to God or will you continue to defy Him?" The Angel faded from sight.

The Admiral was stunned. Regardless of his upbringing, his education, and his life of experiences; he knew beyond a shadow of a doubt that the Angel was real, and had felt the fullness of eternity when Caleb touched his arm. He looked like he was about to collapse and his Aide grabbed his arm and helped him to sit down. Jack went to a refrigerator and got him some water.

After a few minutes he regained his composure and spoke rapid Chinese to his Aide who responded in kind. Finally, the Admiral turned to Jack. "Pardon me; I am very shocked by the Angel's visit. I needed to seek some balance after that."

Jack nodded his head, "Perfectly understandable, Admiral. We deal on an almost daily interaction with Angels, demons, and other supernatural beings. You never really get used to it."

The Admiral smiled, "I see, but I have an additional burden in that my country, my government, and my family are all ignorant of this reality and will not tolerate my new understanding."

Jack spoke to the man in High Mandarin; "I see that your associate feels as you do. Perhaps you both can leave this occurrence out of your records to prevent trouble?"

The Admiral shook his head, "we are both wearing body cameras with audio pickups that are relayed to my ship. What I've seen and heard is already part of the record. I am afraid that my career is over."

Jack nodded, "Just a minute." He got up and called Ethan Reaper, "Ethan, the admiral and his Aide both have body cams with sound, can you do anything to remove the last ten minutes of the recorded history on their ship?"

Ethan checked and responded, "Afraid not Jack, I could wipe the whole thing but it would be pretty obvious we had done it."

Jack was in a quandary, he knew that Vice Chairman Tangtao could help the Admiral but that could reveal his Christianity and lose him his position and most likely his life. But, he didn't want the Admiral to lose either. So he prayed for God's guidance in this matter. He felt reassurance and peace concerning the problem. He had enough experience that he was able to go back to the Admiral and assure him that their recordings would not reveal their Heavenly interactions.

The Admiral was pleased and took his farewell with gratitude. Later, he called to thank Jack for his visit and implied that neither his nor his Aide's recordings worked. The Chinese technicians felt it was the lining of the hull on the Sword that prevented the recordings. Jack knew it wasn't that; but, most likely an Angel messing with all the recordings.

# CHAPTER FORTY-FOUR

Mark sat back in his chair in the War Room and asked Jack and Laura, "Do you guys remember when we were battling demons outside the Hiram Windsor pavilion north of London?" When they both confirmed that they remembered he continued. "Remember at the end of the battle when Rob chain-gunned the demons from the "Formidable" and ended the assault?" Two more nods from Jack and Laura. "Well, something has bothered me since then and I'm just coming to terms with it now. The demons attacked Rob through a portal they opened up on the flight deck of the plane to get at him. I was under the impression that it took roughly fifteen minutes for them to establish a locus to open a portal, right?" More nods.

"How could they get a locus that moved with the plane?"

Jack thought about that and spoke into the air, "Raquel?"

With a whirling flash of gold and fierce white the Angel Rose appeared. "How can I help you Jack? Raquel is busy right now."

Jack outlined Mark's question to Rose who looked at him for several seconds. "I will ask Hugo this question. It is beyond my ability to answer you." She faded out of sight.

Laura sighed, "I don't believe I've ever seen Rose so puzzled before".

A few minutes later Rose reappeared. "Hugo wants to talk to you about this. I don't recall him ever being stumped by a question like this before now."

The three of them suddenly found themselves in a quiet Heavenly setting in a great hall that stretched for several thousand yards in length and a hundred feet tall. The hall was made of a pearl-like substance and had a lot of rugs and many colored tapestries hanging on the walls.

Hugo appeared and studied the three of them. All at once; Sarah, David, Alexis, and Christi appeared with them. Hugo motioned all of them to adjourn to an area with chairs and couches which hadn't been there before.

Once everyone was seated, Hugo sat with them. His wise face with the alert eyes smiled. "Well, well, leave it to you people to pose a question that upset the flow of harmony for the majority of Heaven." Seeing the concerned looks on several faces he quickly reassured them, "Not that there is anything wrong with asking the question."

"The problem is that they should not have been able to do that. The inter-dimensional portal was created for a much more peaceful purpose than a means of attack for embodied demons. It was also created to be used by humans in a different time for travel between the Heavenly and the Earthly dimensions. That Satan would pervert it to transport his embodied demon spirits came as no surprise to anyone. That is what he does and he originally wanted it so he could sneak into heaven. The Most High slammed that door permanently closed and sealed before he could use it for that purpose. It was also designed only for one geostatic point on Earth and one point in Heaven. The problem you have brought to light is that it is being used to allow the insertion of embodied demons to destinations such as ships at sea and now, aircraft in flight."

Hugo saw incomprehension on the human's faces. "Don't you see? The basic design has been modified! Satan and his demons are incapable of original thought! As are we Angels also. They could not have modified the basic design of the inter-dimensional portal to do these things. Someone else must be aiding them. Worse yet, that person must be in Heaven because the portal design requires access and understanding of three dimensions not available to Earth."

Laura asked, "Hugo, how can it be someone in Heaven? God would not do this, God would not allow anyone in Heaven that was less than true and obedient, and the Angels aren't any more creative than Satan is."

Hugo nodded, "I understand your viewpoint my dear. But there are other forces in other dimensions of the Heavenly realm than Angels and humans. You are not aware of things of this nature and they are not for you to worry about. This falls to God and He will resolve all concerns about it."

Hugo and the great hall faded from sight and the original trio found themselves back in the War Room on the Sword.

Jack shrugged his shoulders, "Hugo is right, again, this is definitely above our pay grade."

# CHAPTER FORTY-FIVE

Jack checked on the progress of Rob Maxwell, the Design Labs leader and their "Formidable" pilot. He checked Rob's schedule and went to the basic sword training class. Rob was struggling with the techniques and obviously stressed out. Jack asked Su Li how he was doing overall in his training.

She shrugged her shoulders, "He's trying really hard but seems to believe that his age is an insurmountable problem. He's never had any combat classes before and doesn't know how to get his head into the idea of fighting for his life. I think he needs to understand the concept of a one-on-one fight to the death. Think you can motivate him?"

"Probably, but I know a couple of people that can do a better job than I can. Why don't you cut him loose to me and let us see what can be done?"

Su Li halted Rob's practice and had him store his wooden sword and bow off the practice mat.

Jack greeted him and took him up to the dining area for a soft drink. After they were seated Jack asked him, "How are your classes going?"

Bob smiled, "I think I'm doing fairly well in all my classes except this one. I think I'm too old to get the routines like the younger students. I hate to let you down Jack but, it seems beyond me somehow.

Jack smiled back," Well, you are the second oldest student to learn sword fighting from scratch. I don't know if you know it or not but before starting up the Crossfire Team I was a teacher in Marital Arts, including sword fighting. I teach some advanced techniques here also." Rob shook his head, "No, I didn't know that."

Jack sat back, "I feel I'm a pretty good judge of raw talent and I think you have the makings of a great swordsman. I also know that God is a perfect judge of talent and He was the one that agreed that you were a good candidate for this job."

Rob looked happy that the Lord had picked him.

Jack nodded, "And I know the perfect teacher for you too. He trained all of the swords people here, including me."

Jack bowed his head and prayed for heavenly help. In an eye blink He and Rob were in Heaven sitting across from Hugo. Jack started to explain when Hugo held up his hand stopping him. "It's alright Jack, I scheduled extra time in advance because I knew you would have new people for me to train. Now Rob, I'm Hugo and I am going to train you properly for sword fighting. Forget about being too old, I'm going to give you a new attitude as well as teaching you to be an expert fighter. After all, I'm a teacher of experts and I'm over six thousand years old and it hasn't slowed me down. Hugo looked at Rob for a short while and then asked him, "Are you ready to learn how to wield a sword?"

Rob seemed like a different person, "You bet Hugo, let's get started!" He got up and paced away stretching his arms.

Hugo quietly told Jack, "It really wasn't that he lacked will, but he had a spirit of failure latched onto him telling him he could never master sword fighting. I just cleaned up his mind and put in a real surprise for that little demon when Rob is back in his body. He will do well."

Jack frowned, "Why couldn't I detect that spirit? I mean I am the priest for the team."

Hugo nodded, "That one is a deceptive spirit that hides carefully and doesn't do big things just so he won't be found. Next time you find a willing person stymied and unable seek God for the reason. It could well be one like this. Keep refining your senses and you'll start finding them. Now, this may take a while with Rob although he won't lose much elapsed time on Earth. You might as well go back now." As Hugo faded out Jack thought "If I'd thought to ask, I could have learned some too."

Captain Conners called Jack and Mark up to the bridge, when they arrived he led them over to the plot board. "We have a potential situation coming up that worries me."

Jack noted that the emphasis was on the "worries me" instead of the Captain's normal "concerns me".

Jack nodded, "Show us what the situation is."

The Captain pointed to five red indicators, three just ahead of their path and two more behind them. "These are all submarines, hunter-killer subs, all belonging to Russia. No signals and no warnings. The best estimate your Major Reaper can give us is that they've used this arrangement three times before and each time it was for attacking another submarine. The Major also indicates that it is an attack formation in their secret fleet instruction manual. Once they reach an equal distance from the target they each fire four of their latest version of high speed torpedoes."

Mark asked, is the Force Generator on?"

The Captain nodded. Jack said, "Let's pray and see what God wants us to do." The three men bowed their heads and prayed for wisdom.

Mark looked up. "Oh man, I did not expect that after the spy boat incident."

Jack looked at the Captain, "All right, Captain you can consider God's Word as the ultimate command. Make it happen."

The Captain nodded, "Yes Sir! XO give me a plot for a collision course at the highest possible speed for all five attackers, right now!"

Hugh Kelly didn't flinch, "Aye, aye Sir!"

In the next five minutes he reported back. "Captain, the plot is laid in. The first three where they are and a short tail chase for the other two submarines who will attempt to escape and evade. I assume you intend to take out all five of the enemy completely."

The Captain's face was set. "God himself doesn't want any survivors. Execute the counter attack immediately after their torpedoes detonate."

"Aye, aye, Sir"

The XO added, "Do you want us to blanket any communications by the enemy, Sir?"

Mark spoke to the Captain. He relayed the information. "No I don't XO. They probably have observers nearby lying doggo anyway. Let Mother Russia hear what she has reaped as a caution against trying it in the future."

Jack told Ethan to let everyone on the team see what was about to happen along with the note that God has ordered it.

Hugh Kelly said, "Three minutes to show time."

The three minutes went by agonizingly slow. At the precise minute all five Russian submarines launched four torpedoes at the Sword. Twenty-five seconds later all of the torpedoes detonated against the Force Generator field.

Hugh Kelly ordered the counter attack maneuver. All though there was no sensation inside the Sword, the world outside the ship as seen through the view screens accelerated to a very high speed and the ship turned right and then arced to the left. As predicted, the Sword slammed through the three submarines one by one, two directly in front of the conning tower and the third one twenty feet aft of the conning tower as it accelerated to escape destruction. It didn't matter; the collision was a catastrophic ripping off of the back third of the sub and led to total destruction with a loss of all hands.

The Sword had continued to build speed and headed toward the rear attackers at over one hundred knots. Before the first submarine could cover a quarter mile of escape the Sword ran over it from behind collapsing the back half and slitting the conning tower and front end of the sub into two parts. The last submarine was running west at its highest speed when the Sword caught up with it. The sub tried to maneuver away but was caught anyway and it suffered the same fate as the one before it.

As the debris and bodies fell out of the wreck, Hugh told the Captain, "Sir, counter attack is complete. I have the location of the observer craft; shall I deal with it too?"

"No XO, we've done what God ordered and Russia needs to hear what happens when you try to kill God's warriors. Let us give all the glory to God for the victory!"

Jack quietly asked Mark, "How many personnel were in those five subs?"

Mark shook his head, "Most likely those were all fourth-generation Borei class HKs with a crew of 107, made up of 55 Officers and 52 enlisted men. Times five means we just wiped out a third of that whole class of submarines and five hundred and thirty-five crew. Worse than that, we just eliminated three billion, eight hundred and fifty million dollars of precious Russian capitol. I'm pretty sure we've added Russia to our short list of the OWG and China as our three prime earthly enemies.

Jack looked at his best friend and shrugged his shoulders. "We know that God doesn't make mistakes and this was his plan."


The Crossfire Team will return in:
***"Far East Crossfire"***

If this story has awakened you or moved you to seek the love of Christ and His power for your life, whether you've never accepted Jesus as your savior or you've fallen away, repeat the following prayer and begin a most wonderful journey into eternal life with Him today.

Father God in heaven, As You said in Your Holy Word, (Romans 10:9) that if we confess the Lord Jesus as our God and believe in our hearts that by His Holy Spirit Yahveh God raised Jesus from the dead, we shall be saved.

(The prayer on the next page is a sample prayer when asking Jesus into your heart as your Savior. You can also pray this in your own words.)

# Salvation Prayer

*Dear God in heaven, I come to you in the name of Jesus. I confess to You that I am a sinner, and I am sorry for my sins and the life that I have lived; I need your forgiveness. I believe that your only begotten Son Jesus Christ shed His precious blood on the cross at Calvary and died for my sins, and I am now willing to turn from my sin.*

*Right now I confess Jesus as the Lord of my life and my soul. With all my heart, I truly believe that your Holy Spirit raised Jesus from the dead. Today I accept Jesus Christ as my personal Savior and according to Your Word, right now I am saved.*

*I thank you Jesus, for your unlimited grace which has saved me from my sins. I thank you Jesus that your grace that never leads to license, but rather it always leads to repentance. Therefore Lord Jesus, transform my life so that I may bring glory and honor to you alone and not to myself.*

*I thank you Lord Jesus, for shedding Your blood in seven different places to restore me in this life and for dying for me at Calvary and giving me eternal life.*

*Amen.*

If you just said this prayer and you meant it with all your heart, believe that you are now saved and have been born again.

You may ask, "Now that I am saved, what do I do next?" First of all you need to get into a spirit-filled, bible-based church that teaches the Scriptures, and you need to study God's Word.

Once you have found a church home, you will want to become water-baptized by immersion. By accepting Christ you are baptized in the spirit, but it is through water-baptism that you publically announce your obedience to the Lord Jesus. Water baptism is a symbol of your salvation from the dead. You were dead but now you live, for Jesus Christ has redeemed you for a price! The price was His atoning death on the cross. May God Bless You as you learn to walk in His light!